The Sexbot

The Sexbot

J. Boyett

SALTIMBANQUE BOOKS

NEW YORK

Typeset by Christopher Boynton

Saltimbanque Books, New York
www.saltimbanquebooks.com
jboyett.net

ISBN: 978-1-941914-14-4

For Leo and Mary.

For Chris Boyett, Pam Carter, Dawn Drinkwater,
and Andy Shanks.

Acknowledgments

Once again, Kelly Kay Griffith's generosity, intelligence, and taste were invaluable.

The Sexbot

One

While waiting for the taxi Brad tried to simultaneously access the school portal and hold the half-broken umbrella over his children. His wet fingers kept scrambling commands as he swiped them across the damp screen. Finally, he called up Katie's profile; "Katie, you fibbed to me about your quiz grade!"

Katie shoved her brother Keith out of the protective circle of the umbrella and into the drizzle. He shrieked. Katie was nine years old, Keith seven. Brad grabbed her arm and shook it—that made him lose his grip on the umbrella and drop his tablet.

The taxi arrived and they climbed into its blue-and-white plastic shell. Brad told the AI their destination, then eyed the map displayed on the back of the seat to make sure the program hadn't garbled his request, and that the blinking dot of their destination was indeed the kids' school. A dinging noise demanded that he pay the fare in advance. He almost didn't hear the dinging over the jingles and cheery voices of the multiple ads displayed on the taxi's other screens (you could tap the screens to silence them, but since they'd just come on a second later, forcing you to tap again, it wasn't worth the trouble). Brad's car was in the shop. The locking mechanism was on the fritz, and none of its doors could be opened; he'd had to pay to get it towed so that a programmer could look at it.

Brad continued scolding Katie for her grades. "But school is *boring*!" she protested.

Undoubtedly true. Katie was a bright girl. "I know this school isn't advanced enough for you," he said. "But you'll never get into a better one if you don't make good grades here."

"I don't wanna be in one at *all*," she muttered.

The taxi hydroplaned and Brad froze till it regained traction. "Buckle up, kids!" he said.

The taxi pulled up to the drop-off zone in front of the elementary school's main campus. Screaming kids teemed beneath the covered walkway. The school had long since outgrown its original building, and Katie and Keith would only be here half the day before being shuttled to a satellite campus. Brad double-checked on his tablet that they each had enough in their school accounts to cover the toll.

He hugged Keith goodbye, then Katie, holding her an extra few seconds. "I know it's hard at school," he said. "Just try, and I'll try, too, to figure out a way to make it better." She kept her face blank till he released her, then burst away from him. Keith had already run ahead, his tablet in his hands, playing a video game as he went.

Brad watched them go: Keith bobbing along almost comically, Katie marching with her shoulders hunched up, her long scraggly hair trailing the air behind her.

The door slid shut automatically once Brad drew his limbs back into the car. It only stuck for a moment; Brad slapped the door back onto its tracks.

He told the taxi the address of his job. As the car drove itself through the slick streets of Meerville, Brad closed his eyes; he needed to get into the right headspace. His square face relaxed, but lines of strain remained etched into it, incongruous with his boyishness. By the time the taxi dropped him off the drizzle had paused.

He worked at an honest-to-God indoor mall. Four years ago, during the so-called Rebirth of the Mall, the cavernous old structure had been refurbished, and a dozen stores had been persuaded to rent space inside. Now there were five stores left. When Brad had started working here a year ago there had still been seven.

Of course, his job didn't have much to do with the mall. That was just where it happened to be.

The building's automatic doors still worked, though they slid open with a chronic scratching sound. Nobody was visible in the empty sweep of the first floor, but he heard shouts and

4

laughter echoing from the balcony ringing the second, plus the usual strident bass-heavy music thudding tinnily out of the clothing store. You could hear the clothing store's music throughout the whole building. Above him the skylights towered. He always found himself reluctantly stirred by the vast space, like a crappy cathedral. A thin film of grime layered the linoleum floor. Plastic cups and bags lay here and there, like sleeping homeless people. The escalator still didn't work. Brad climbed it like a staircase to the second-floor balcony ringing the interior. When he got to the second floor, he saw a group of six young black guys gathered around a couple of beat-up old benches, just hanging out and goofing off, talking loud. As he walked by them on his way to the clothing store, he nodded at them briefly, as if they all worked together here at the mall. They eyed him with hostile amusement.

Brad knew that these black guys resented him because he was a white guy and America was so racist. He would have liked to assure them that he knew where they were coming from, and also that things weren't that much better for him. Obviously there was no way he could say any of that.

He entered the clothing store and pretended to browse. The clothes were aimed at kids younger and hipper than Brad, which was ridiculous because the designs weren't hip at all. Brad supposed people his own age might think they were. But they didn't fool him, because he could see with his own eyes what young hip people actually wore.

After idly browsing he headed toward the back, and the dressing rooms. He tried to be discreet. Not that it mattered; the chubby Latina teenager entrusted with the store slouched forward against the counter, head bowed over her tablet. She was watching a video with the volume on high. Its soundtrack sliced through the store's loud music. Employees probably worked in four-hour part-time shifts, and the store must have massive turnover. Jobs might be scarce, but that didn't mean it was worthwhile to keep one that didn't pay enough to cover the costs of your commute. Brad rarely saw the same cashier twice.

He turned the corner into the short hallway with the dressing rooms. As always, no customers. The scuff marks on the white walls showed up well under the glare of the fluorescents. He passed the dressing rooms and came to a much more solid door, bearing a sign: MALL PERSONNEL ONLY. He slipped his card through the magnetic reader. A lock mechanism inside the door clicked. Brad opened the door, leaning into it, and stepped into the brothel antechamber.

As he undressed in the tiny sliver of a room, he called up the client details on the wall monitor. He had read the profile this morning, naturally, while Katie and Keith brushed their teeth, but he liked to refresh.

The first client was a woman, seeking sex with a man. She had marked the "Vanilla" preference box. In his private life, Brad also was a heterosexual Vanilla. Not that that made any difference, when he put on the suit.

From the wall-mounted dispenser he pulled handfuls of sanitizing wipes and scrubbed his nude body. It aided the bonding action of the suit. He slid his card down a second magnetic lock, and stepped out of the antechamber and into the suit room.

A locker had already opened and extended a thin robotic arm from which his suit hung. When he took the suit the arm retracted and the locker closed. He thought of the suit room as the brothel proper, but it had no more claim to that title than the room where the client awaited, wherever that might be. In fact that room had a better claim, since both the client and the utterly lifelike sexbot were there, and that was where the physical interaction would actually take place.

He squeezed himself into the suit's dark gray, rubber-like material. His suit was already meticulously tailored, but putting it on woke up circuitry woven into its fibers, circuitry which molded the garment to become absolutely form-fitting. (The amazingly precise tailoring was what reassured Brad that his suit belonged to him alone, and was not shared among other contractors. No doubt there were other operators' suits tucked away inside the locker. But the contract with Kaufmann-Berlini forbade any contractor to hang out in the vicinity of the v-brothel when not working, or attempt to contact any other contractor or even confirm said contractors' existences.) He adjusted his penis into the elastic condom sheath, arranged his testicles in the sack fitted to his scrotum. Bent over and touched his toes to make sure that the ridges pressing against the rim of his anus, used to simulate the action of a penis in a vagina, were snugly and correctly positioned, even though he would be inhabiting a male body having sex with a female today and therefore wouldn't need them. (Depending on the context, the same ridges simulated a penis in a rectum.) A tube ran from the suit to the wall—when his role was that of a woman, it filled pouches in the suit lining with a paste, to mimic the curvaceous body shape of the female sexbot. Of course, when the client, say, massaged the breasts of the female sexbot, or sucked the sexbot's nipple, those sensations could not be transmitted back to Brad exactly as a woman would process them, because he had no nerves running through the fatty paste in the breast pouches. Finely calibrated pressure cushions and suction nodes approximated those sensations upon his own pectorals, his own nipples. Then it was up to him and his brain to interpret those sensations as erogenous pleasure located in a female body. Countless adjustments like this had to be made over the course of each session. The ability to do so reliably was what made Brad good at his job.

Not one person in a thousand could do what he did.

More than a hundred tiny robots studded the suit's exterior—when Brad affixed the mask, sealing its mouthpiece around the curves of his lips, the robots would leave the suit and skitter across the room, a wire extending out from each one to the suit, each one affixing itself onto the walls, floors, or ceiling. They tracked the distant physical interactions between the sexbot and the client. The coordinated action of the tugging wires, along with the body-temperature pressure pouches embedded throughout the fabric of the suit, would basically reproduce any tugging or pushing that Brad's sexbot avatar received from the client. In Brad's v-brothel location was a raised cushioned slab upon which to fuck, exactly like that in the client's location. Waiting at attention were three robots, a little like hat-racks, one of which bore a body-temperature baton that imitated a penis, the second a warm soft wet paddle that approximated a tongue, and the third bearing a box with a penis-sized hole, containing another tongue-like appendage and lined with artificial lips, able to simulate the suction of a blow job. The client, of course, was not directly hooked up to body-motion sensors, but her or his brothel location was filled with hundreds of cameras and microphones that would transmit his or her motion back to the suit's circuitry, letting it know when to activate which pressure pads, and to the room's circuitry, letting it know when to tug at Brad with the wires, and what to do with the penis baton or tongue paddle. If Brad needed to give a blow job (not that that would happen this session, since the client was female), the baton robot in Brad's location would move into the appropriate position, matching the position of the client's penis in the other location. The position of the client's tongue, of course, could not be determined by cameras, because each tongue generally remained in either the client's or the sexbot's mouth. Therefore the client drank a preparation before the session. Within the preparation were nanobots that spread themselves throughout the mouth's interior, transmitting back to the tongue-paddle in Brad's room the position of the client's tongue, to allow for more sensitive kissing, and a more perfect transmission of information should the client wish to perform oral sex. After an hour the nanobots, never perceptible, would cease functioning, release themselves from the client's tongue and inner cheeks, and be harmlessly swallowed. The suit automatically injected similar nanobots into Brad's mouth, to guide the sexbot's tongue.

He finished suiting up. The stereoscopic VR goggles slid over his eyes. The earbuds went into his ears. Brad stood there in brief but total sensory deprivation, waiting for the new reality to flicker on, for the 3-D video and sound to activate, waiting to meet the client.

Two

He realized something was wrong. Because he felt the feminizing pouches filling with paste. Breasts' gravity tugged at his chest. His ass and hips were swelling.

Shit. Either the client was not a heterosexual woman, but instead a heterosexual man or a lesbian, or else the fuck-up went in the other, more serious direction and the client was going to be confronted with a sexbot of unwanted gender. Fuck. What else had gotten garbled? What if the clients' tastes turned out to *not* be vanilla?

Some part-time data-input prole had screwed up. But it was Brad who would face the anger if the client had a bad time, Brad who would get the bad reviews and see his ratings collapse. Who would lose out on repeat visits from this client. Who would be bypassed by new clients, scrolling through reviews of sexbot operators. It was the data-entry prole who had screwed up, but that was natural because he had a shit job that he hated, so why should he care if he got himself fired? But Brad couldn't afford that. He had one of the last decently-paying skilled jobs out there. Even if everything was the data-entry prole's fault, it was Brad who had to fix it.

A blinking red asterisk in the bottom right corner of his vision alerted him that the client's reality was about to flow into place.

It faded in. Before Brad sat a thin, flabby, balding man. He wore nothing but tidy-whities and thick spectacles. Beside him on the blue plastic bench were his clothes, neatly folded and stacked. Usually the client was either still dressed or already completely nude. Brad intuited that this guy had taken off most of his clothes, then stopped, uncertain whether that was what he ought to do. But he'd second-guessed himself yet again before he could put his clothes back on.

Brad watched the client. He didn't seem discombobulated at being confronted with the female sexbot; although it was hard to say for sure because he did seem *generally* discombobulated. The profile had said he was a first-time customer. Obviously everything the profile said was now in doubt, but Brad believed that detail.

Weirdly, Brad had the impression he'd seen this guy before. But he'd certainly never been Brad's client.

The client blinked at him. He was more haggard than Brad had at first noticed, the flesh sagging from his neck and jawline as if it had grown prematurely weary of hanging on. "Is there … someone in there?"

"Yes!" said Brad, in the cheerful voice that was his default when servicing a hetero male, until and unless he perceived that the client would prefer something else. He stepped forward, to within a foot and a half of where the client sat on the bench. Didn't touch him yet; didn't leer, either; just smiled down in innocent friendliness, letting the body do the talking. As Brad looked at the client past the mounds of the sexbot's perfect breasts, he could see the expanding bulge in the tidy-whities. About a five-inch erection, he guessed, once it established itself.

Blinking heavily, the client tried to maintain polite eye contact even as the sexbot's breasts repeatedly dragged his gaze back. Brad broadened his smile. "Would you like to play with me?" A happy demeanor and a direct approach blew these perennial nice guys to shambles. No hint of exploitation, no doubts about consent.

The client's eyebrows came together almost as if he were in pain and he made a sound like a whispered moan. His blinking increased as his eyes moistened. Trembling, he rose.

Brad couldn't help stepping back a pace. He hadn't had the chance to get into the headspace for this body; unlike the male sexbot, the female model was smaller than him. Therefore, the sight of the client that the VR code transmitted was

10

proportionally large, and because Brad hadn't prepped himself, the man seemed like a giant.

The client caught the startled movement. Stricken, he cried, "I'm sorry! Did I do something wrong?" Frightened of his own masculinity. Secretly convinced that his sexuality was nothing but locked-up implicit violence, a seed that must never be allowed to sprout. A product of the dregs of Judeo-Christian morality and a dumbed-down, bastardized version of third-wave feminism. Brad knew the type. That was why the client had come to a brothel: to have a professional take it all out of his hands. If it was out of his hands then he couldn't be held responsible; if he wasn't responsible then he couldn't be sinning, or exploiting.

"No, no," said Brad. He tried to laugh, bright and tinkling. It came out painfully fake. "It's my fault." True.

The client stood, blinking, distressed, slouch-shouldered, aware of his own absurdity in his tidy-whites. His erection had deflated. He was probably too nice to leave a bad review, but Brad doubted he was going to be a repeat customer.

But the reviews, the money, none of that was the point. Brad prided himself in his work. He didn't want to screw up.

He knew he'd seen this guy before. Then, abruptly, he remembered where: this was the guidance counselor at Katie's and Keith's school!

The realization must have manifested itself somehow on Brad's face, and therefore the sexbot's. Whatever the expression, the client interpreted it as disgust, or anger, or shame, or mockery, or something in that family. Brad saw the hurt in his face before he threw up walls to hide it. Moving toward his clothes, he said, "I'm sorry, I'll still pay, but maybe I should just, you know...."

Brad's heart squeezed, like it was under the wheels of a truck. Then, inspired: "No, *I'm* sorry," he insisted. "It's just, this is, uh, kind of my first time."

Sure enough, the client stopped short. "Oh?" The shame and trouble were briefly washed from his face. Understanding replaced them.

"Yeah." Brad blushed. The micro-sensors in his suit fabric detected it, and somewhere, miles away in another room with the client, the sexbot blushed too. "I'm not supposed to tell you that. So, uh, please don't tell anybody I did." Surely the client would realize, if he thought about it, that AIs were monitoring their interaction to make sure the sexbot operator stayed within certain parameters. But Brad gambled that he wouldn't want to think about it.

"No, of course." As Brad had expected, even though the client's fear of his own ridiculousness had been moved aside by Brad's confession of vulnerability, it was replaced by the fear of his own violence. Having sex with a seasoned professional was one thing, but breaking someone's cherry was another. "I mean, maybe in that case…. I mean, if you're not sure, then I don't think you should, you know…."

"No." Brad stepped forward, clasped the client's hand in his own. "I'd like you to be first. You seem like a good person."

"No, well, I mean, you don't know me or anything…."

"I just feel like I can trust you, is all. I don't know why."

"Well, I mean."

Brad straightened the arm of the hand that was holding the client's hand. That had the effect of bringing them closer together, and of pressing the sexbot's warm breasts against the client's arm. The client's breathing got heavier. Still, he kept himself from letting go just yet, and peered into the sexbot's eyes, squinting, as if to see through them to the unknown operator miles away.

Brad gently pinched the head of the client's penis through the white cloth of his underwear, and tickled his fingers up the shaft. The client's eyes rolled back as his lids fluttered.

Brad stood on his tiptoes and put his mouth to the client's mouth. He still hadn't managed to hypnotize himself into thinking he was only a bit over five feet, and couldn't help perceiving the client as seven feet tall, thanks to the proportional compensations effected by the VR at his end.

As his tongue left the client's mouth, he said, "So, now you know it's my first time. So if I do anything you'd like me to do different then just please, you know, tell me." He infused the words with frightened vulnerability, then smothered that with brazen self-confidence.

As planned, the client saw through the self-confidence to the vulnerability Brad had planted underneath. His face, which had become thick and stupid with desire, cleared and became serious, almost noble, as he took a second look into the sexbot's eyes. "Don't worry. You're gonna do great."

This was awesome. Brad had been knocked off-guard upon finding himself inhabiting the wrong gender. But he'd managed to sell that loss of poise as his own case of the jitters. That had given the client a chance to find his protective, patriarchal side, which was what he really wanted—no doubt he believed he'd come for debauched pleasure, but what he'd *really* come for was to be a Man. He just happened to believe that the lusty, uncaring pursuit of hedonistic pleasure was the only type of Manhood open to him. He hadn't dared imagine he'd find access to this more old-fashioned, idealized template of Manhood.

If you can fulfill a desire that the client doesn't even know he or she has, and which he or she still can't define even after having experienced its fulfillment, then your odds of getting a follow-up appointment are high. Barring certain psychological problems on the client's part.

The client insisted on cunnilingus; probably he thought it the gentlemanly thing to do. On Brad's end, the suit translated the client's lapping of the sexbot's vagina into the sensations of an uninspired, loose-lipped, occasionally painful blow job. Since he was having sex as a woman instead of a man, the option to fake his enjoyment was more feasible; when playing a man, if his real penis lost its erection then so would the sexbot's; as a female, his erection did influence such factors as vaginal lubrication, but he could fake an orgasm with the same relative ease as any other woman. Yet Brad would have considered that a personal defeat. His job was to give the client pleasure: pleasure centered in the client's body, but also his own pleasure, his own real pleasure in the creation of which he guided his partner, the client. There were too few non-bullshit jobs left in the world for him not to take his own seriously.

The trick was to feel not what the client was really doing, but what the client *intended* to do. Brad closed his eyes and imagined himself in the client's body, munching away. Perhaps the client even realized he was doing a clumsy job. But there was still something he was munching his way toward: some rippling pool of crystal pleasures hidden in the dark strange cave. Brad visualized those pleasures along with the client. Dreamed of arriving at them, just as the client did. Leaning back on the cushioned slab, eyes closed, Brad's jaw and tongue made shadow movements, lightly aping the client's. They pursued that place together. And together, they arrived. Brad let out sharp cries as the pleasure spilled out and flooded his being. The suit injected a hormone into his blood to keep him erect after orgasm, so that he could attain multiple orgasms, as the ideal woman would do. It was one of the few direct, biological interventions the suit ever made.

After Brad came, he lay the client out on the cushioned slab there in the room with the sexbot. Then Brad got on all fours on the table himself, orientating the sexbot's body so that its ass and vagina were available to the client's hands and mouth, should he wish to manipulate those areas while Brad performed oral sex. The client grabbed and stroked the buttocks and made a nervous foray into the vagina with his forefinger, before becoming too preoccupied to do anything but grip the buttocks hard and gasp. Brad miscalculated, delivering such an intense blow job that the client nearly came too early, which would have made him feel foolish. Brad took his time languorously changing position, in order to give the client a chance to get himself under control; then he drew the client down on top of him. He could tell that what the client really wanted was to be mounted by the sexbot, but if they did so right away the client would orgasm too soon.

Soon, though, Brad switched from missionary to cowgirl. The sexbot mounted the actual client, while, in the suit room, the wires held Brad suspended over the client's phantom body, in the exact same position as the sexbot. Rocking atop a client worked well for Brad. A ring of inflating and deflating cushions bumped against the rim of his anus in order to approximate the action of the client's penis in the sexbot's vagina, and somehow the pressure seemed more aptly placed when Brad rode a client or when he was on all fours being taken from behind, than it did when he was on his back, say, as in missionary. The ring did not go deep enough to affect his prostate, or anything like that. It was just a cue as to what sort of sensations he should provide to the phantom vagina and clitoris he'd conjured in his mind. (When the sexbot, male or female model, was on the receiving end of anal sex, this pounding ring worked with greater force and insistence, but never did it push its way into his anus proper; Brad's work never had any profound effect upon his personal body; the company had promised that, and since Brad was a heterosexual man without extreme sexual tastes, he would have insisted on such a condition.)

In the lower left-hand corner of his vision, Brad saw that they were nearing the half-hour mark. He went ahead and brought the client to orgasm; the guy had had a great lay, and Brad figured he would want a little after-glow chatting. Sometimes Brad could sense that a client, male or female, had zero interest in small talk, in which case he tried to stretch the sexual activity out to the end of their session. But that was rare. After all, they'd paid quite a bit extra for the human-interaction component. Kaufmann-Berlini, the company that owned the v-brothels, offered a much cheaper sexbot-only option. And if they'd wanted nothing but the body stuff, lots of folks could have afforded to save up and buy their own sexbot. There were plenty of open-source programs on the internet, that could get the machine to do whatever knocked your socks off.

But very few AIs would have been sensitive enough to turn that gender screw-up into an advantage, the way he had. Brad indulged in a little self-praise.

They cuddled. "How much time do I have?" asked the client.

Brad checked the clock in the lower left corner of his vision. "Four minutes, technically. But we can take our time."

"Oh, really? There's no one else who ... um, you know...."

"We're fine." More than an hour remained until the next session. May as well take advantage of the lull to cultivate this guy a bit. The sex had been good enough that Brad was already hopeful he'd get a repeat, but it couldn't hurt to reinforce. "There's time."

"In that case...." The client scrambled off the slab, rummaged something out of the knapsack under his folded clothes, and returned to once more cuddle against Brad with an electronic cigarette in hand. He was about to turn it on and inhale, then lowered it, seeming embarrassed. "Sorry. Never mind."

"You can vape," said Brad, surprised.

"No, it's fine. I basically never do it, I just was going to because...." He laughed nervously. "Because guys in movies and stuff always smoke after making love to someone, and I wanted to see what it's like."

"Oh. Well, if you change your mind, don't worry about me."

"Okay. I'm Duane, by the way."

"It's nice to meet you, Duane. You can call me Becky."

"That's not your real name, though, right?" Again Duane laughed nervously, at his own daring in posing the question. Brad just smiled kindly, via the sexbot.

Duane cleared his throat. "But, though, is it possible for me to ask.... Are you a girl, on the other side of the 'bot? A woman, I mean?"

Brad delivered the first half of his canned answer: "Company policy forbids me to come out and answer that. I'm really sorry, I wish I *could* answer. It might cost me my job, though."

"Right, no, I know all that," Duane said, nodding to assure her it was okay to quit talking, feeling guilty for even having asked.

Brad delivered the canned answer's second half: "*Officially*, I can't tell you which gender. But unofficially ... do you really think a man could make love the way I just did?"

"No." Relief spilled across Duane's face as if it were being released from a broken abscess. "But so ... I mean, sometimes you have to act like a man, right? That's what I read. What is that like?"

It was great that Duane was a nice guy. It made him easier to handle. But it did pose its own challenges. He might be kind and polite enough to take an interest in Brad, but it behooved Brad to discourage Duane from dwelling on "Becky's" life outside their sessions, and especially from picturing "her" operating a male sexbot and servicing some woman, or, worse, some homosexual man. "I'd rather hear about you," he said. A lame sally, but for accompaniment he tickled his finger along the line of Duane's bicep.

Duane shrugged. Because Brad was cuddled against his ribs with Duane's arm around him, the shrug moved his whole body. "Nothing to tell." Duane gave Brad a bright, determined look and Brad understood that he was about to dare to say something. It was: "You look like a painting."

Brad smiled. "Thank you! What does that mean? Something good, I hope."

"Yeah. Don't worry. Something good."

Three

Twelve kids bouncing dutifully in a bounce castle. Standing or sitting around the perimeter of its netting, moms and dads hunched their faces over their tablet screens, or smiled exclusively at their own child. They avoided eye contact with each other. Conversation would have been difficult anyway; Cheezy Charly's three-minute theme song blared from the ceiling speakers. When the song finished there would be four minutes of even louder ads. Then the song would begin again.

Brad was one of the standers, not the sitters. That allowed him to be closer to the netting, and to his kids. He smiled encouragement at Katie and Keith as they bounced, rather dourly he thought. They were here because Brad had joined a child-socialization Meetup. The surrounding parents were fellow members. Last Wednesday, Brad had, as usual, promised himself he would go to bed as soon as the kids were tucked in. And as usual, he had instead spent a couple hours aimlessly scrolling through RollSnap, checking out the profiles of family members and other contacts. The post-diet photos of people he'd last seen in high school. Baby vids posted by strangers he must have met but couldn't remember. Pithy lovelife updates posted by women he'd buddied on RollSnap after having met once, without ever getting around to asking them out later. Also the link to yet another article about how children were being brain-damaged by a lack of real-time, face-to-face, non-digital socializing with others their own age. In a panic Brad had minimized the RollSnap window and gone to Meetup.com, where to his relief he'd found a playdate Meetup right here in Meerville.

He scrutinized his children. He had uneasy doubts whether this counted as "socializing," since the kids weren't talking to anyone, just bouncing and staring into space. Then again, it would be weird for Katie and Keith to just start talking to some kid who wasn't even looking at them, so maybe their silence was a sign that they were well-adjusted. Self-sufficient. He tried to give them another encouraging smile but couldn't catch either child's eye.

Checking to make sure no one was looking over his shoulder, Brad accessed his v-brothel portal. Tapped in his long password, and looked to see if he had any upcoming work.

Hey, Duane had booked another appointment! Awesome. It was funny, because Brad had an appointment with Duane the next day—but not as Becky. He'd scheduled a meeting with the guidance counselor to discuss getting Katie into the Pence Academy.

Ever since he was a little kid, Brad had heard talk about how AIs were going to make humans obsolete in pretty much every field. And during his thirty-five years he'd seen it inexorably happen. He'd found himself an air pocket in the rising water; v-brotheling was still a valid means of employment. But what the fuck were his kids going to do? Maybe the Pence Academy would help put them on some path through the muck. It might help *something* happen.

You could never tell what would happen. He'd had to sink to real desperation before it had even occurred to him to try brotheling. And he never would have guessed it would actually work out. In the hours before the audition, he'd been a jangling wreck. Especially when they texted him that he'd be fucking a man, while operating a female sexbot. But then, once he'd put on the suit, once the breast and hip and buttock pouches had begun to swell, a great open stillness had come over him. All that nervousness had belonged to Brad, and Brad wasn't here anymore—this female body was not Brad's. He vividly remembered that first client, though he'd never known much about him. An eager beaver. He'd been expecting a company rep or something, but the guy hadn't had a very professional vibe. Brad knew that from time to time the v-brothels would do promotional lotteries, or raffles with a free fuck as the prize. He imagined the winners were used for these auditions. If the fuck-session were bad, the client hadn't paid anything more than the price of a raffle ticket, so nobody much cared.

He'd gotten lucky with the brotheling. But he couldn't count on the same sort of luck for his children.

He surveyed the other parents here at Cheezy Charly's. Part of the reason he'd joined this Meetup was a fantasy that his children might make friends with some kid out of their sphere, associating with whom could lift them up a rung. But most of these parents struck him as probably having jobs more bullshit than his.

This Meetup was not going to be his kids' ticket into that higher world. The Pence Academy was their best bet. Only bet, maybe.

The school always seemed grimier than Brad remembered his as having been. More trash littering the hallways. Walls scuffed up more, more dents in the lockers. Maybe it was just the more critical eye of adulthood.

He sat in the office, waiting for the appointment with the guidance counselor. Duane. The chair was too small for him. He held his palms pressed together, his hands sandwiched between his thighs. Keeping his body tensed prevented him from fidgeting.

The school's dilapidated state was probably to be expected. It was so much bigger than his own elementary had been. What with all the consolidation, there were over five thousand kids here. It was the most crowded of Meerville's elementary schools. Lots of wear and tear.

Somewhere in this school were Katie and Keith—he'd dropped them off only an hour ago, and it wasn't yet time for them to be shuttled to the satellite campus. He hadn't bothered to tell them he had a meeting here. The odds of them bumping into each other in such a huge place were so slim, he hadn't seen the point of mentioning it.

Brad squeezed his hands even tighter between his knees to prevent his fingers from plucking at each other. Being here brought back childhood fears of being called to the principal's office. It had never actually happened—his fear had kept him in line. Katie, on the other hand, did occasionally get called in for reprimand. Secretly Brad felt a little proud of that. Of her spunk.

The secretary called, "Mr. Tollardson?" She gazed into empty space, as if she were calling out to a crowd and had no idea where this Mr. Tollardson might be, even though Brad was the only visitor and had introduced himself when he'd first arrived, ten minutes ago, seven minutes early. He pulled himself free of the tight chair and stood before the woman's desk. "Mr. Wilkes will see you now," she said, with a vague wave toward the guidance counselor's office. Disapproval stained her face, as if Brad really were a misbehaving student being sent in for his punishment. That was probably the appropriate expression often enough that she didn't feel the need to add another to her repertoire. Brad went into the office, squeezing his sweaty once-white ball cap in both hands before him.

Duane sat at his desk. Mr. Wilkes. He smiled tightly up at Brad, then returned to his tablet and continued fiddling with it. It was weird, seeing him in this constrained and superficial setting so soon after having managed to access some legitimate passion during their sex session. Not as weird as it would have been to someone unaccustomed to Brad's job, though. He understood that his identities when inhabiting the male or female sexbots were not the same as the ones he lived while walking around in his own body. As if he were part of a loose community of quasi-strangers who happened to share a common pool of memories.

"Mr. Tollardson, sit down please." Duane—Mr. Wilkes—said this with surprise and almost embarrassment, upon noticing that Brad seemed too polite to do so without being asked. Brad lowered himself into one of the two chairs facing the desk, aluminum frames upholstered with algae-green pleather. This chair was big enough for him, but it swayed a little as he settled his weight into it, and Brad wondered if it might collapse. Duane's desk was a big aluminum box with a particle-board top, and a plastic sheet glued on to provide a smooth surface. A wood-grain pattern was printed on the plastic sheet.

Duane kept screwing with his tablet a few seconds, then spat out a sigh. "I'm sorry, I know we have a meeting scheduled, but I can't access your son's file to see what it's in regard to."

"It's my daughter, actually. Katie. Katie Maron."

"Oh. Yes. Sorry, guess I was looking under, uh…."

"Yeah, they have their mom's last name. Katie and Keith."

"Right, right." Finally Duane put down the tablet. "Sorry to be distracted. And unprepared."

"No, no. Is there, like, a filing problem, or…?"

"No, it's just the thing is worn out. The school district only replaces the tablets every five years. The touch screen is basically shot, so I have to tap each icon about twenty times before the tablet senses my finger. Except it looks like now not even that works."

It had been a long time since Brad had known of a tablet lasting longer than three years. "Dude, that sucks."

"Oh, it's not so bad," said Duane hastily. Brad understood— Duane had caught himself bitching about his job, and had a sudden fright at what might happen if it got around the office that he was complaining. Got back to the school board, got back to the treasurer, the fiduciary supervisors, the EdDep Rep.

"Since I'm not able to access Katie's file," continued Duane, "would you mind reminding me why we called you in? Assuming you know."

"Actually it was me who requested the meeting."

"Oh. Okay."

"Sorry, I know you're super-busy…."

"No, no, it's great to see a parent taking an interest. What can I help you with?"

Brad cleared his throat shyly. He only had a ten-minute meeting. No time to waste. "Well, I just…. I know there's no reason to expect special treatment. Except Katie *is* special, I feel like. She needs more of, like, a challenge."

Duane looked forlornly at the tablet. Wishing he could access her file, no doubt, instead of taking the dad's word. "She's been having behavioral problems?"

"Acting out. That's all. And ... well, academic problems, too. But, I know this sounds backwards, but her academic problems really do come from the fact that she's too advanced."

"That does happen. Of course, in order to see whether I agree I'd have to check her file, which, for the moment...."

"No, I know. But I think once you do you'll see that, um.... I really think she'd be better off at the Pence Academy."

Duane's face closed up, blocking off all points of access. In its place he hung a mask of sympathetic regret. "Slots for the Pence Academy are competitive...."

"Sure, sure. But that's because the students they let in are advanced. Which is why Katie would fit in. And then as for Keith, I think there's a policy that they also accept at least one sibling of any student they let in...."

"As long as that sibling meets certain standards. Well. Like I said, I'll have to wait till I can get to a reliable computer and check her file before I can honestly evaluate her chances...."

"I think it would help with her socialization, too." Brad was blurting out his whole case. "I've read that proper socialization is really important for development. And I think that stuff would be easier for Katie at Pence Academy, because she'd be around her peers. I mean, don't you feel like socialization is hard, anyway? For any of us?"

"Sure. Um. But, well, if it's hard for everyone, the fact that it's hard for your daughter doesn't necessarily make her special, you see."

Brad felt like he had been dropped into a vat of freezing water. Duane saw his reaction, and cringed. "I didn't mean she's *not* special, I was just making a point...."

"She is special, she really is. Way above average."

"I'm sure that she is." Duane gave his tablet another desperate look, and began once more hopelessly fiddling with it. "I wish

I could access her testing data, to give you an honest opinion of her chances."

Brad knew her Basics score, but he understood that Duane meant the analyses, both more extensive and more granular, that the government and school board had access to. As Duane messed with the unresponsive tablet, Brad took note of the time displayed on its screen. Their ten minutes were almost up.

"Listen," said Brad, "I, uh, I know it's not policy, and I know it's not your fault the tablet doesn't work. And I don't want to put you out or inconvenience you or anything." Duane already looked worried by this preamble. "But I just, ah, I feel kind of weird about you not being able to access Katie's records, you know? And see her scores. It kind of makes it feel like this meeting shouldn't really count."

Nice guy that he was, Duane looked guilty again. As expected. "You're right," he said, "it *is* crappy that the tablet isn't working. But, well, it'll be hard to schedule another meeting before the deadline for Pence Academy recommendations. You know parents are only permitted one requested appointment per semester. But I can assure you that...."

"No, I know all that, and I know you'll be fair in looking over her file. But I still just.... I mean, I know I'm not allowed to book another meeting. But maybe we could just, uh ... meet unofficially? Like, hang out?"

Duane's eyes fluttered down toward the desk, and around the corners of the office. Anywhere that wasn't Brad's eyes. His mouth moved, as if he knew he was supposed to be talking, but couldn't think of what to say.

If it had seemed to Brad like Duane hated the suggestion and was hunting for a polite way out, he would have backed off. But he recognized this brand of embarrassment. He'd already seen it in a more intimate form: it was the look Duane got when he realized some pleasure was in the offing, some pleasure he didn't believe he truly deserved, or was really going to get.

Brad said, "It would just be, like, socializing. There's no rule against that, right? I mean, you're allowed to be friends with the parents, right?" Hearing the word "friends" escape his throat, Brad blushed, feeling he'd been very forward. It was all he could do not to hurriedly take it back.

Duane pursed his lips, tilted his head to one side. "Well. If it really means a lot to you to have our talk, after I've looked over your daughter's full test results...."

"It does. Not that I wouldn't trust you to make a fair decision, without needing to talk to me. But, just, you know."

"No, yeah, I do. Um. Just, at a ... I mean, where should we?..."

"At, I guess, maybe like a bar?..."

"Oh. Okay." Duane thought it over, then nodded; yes, that was the sort of place that would make sense. Like in movies, when people hung out, that was the sort of place they did it at. He cleared his throat and said, "I guess I'll give you my personal e-mail address," a little tentatively, almost certain that was the right thing but with just a hint of doubt, letting Brad have the chance to object in case Duane was doing something untoward. Brad said nothing. He felt grateful that Duane was pulling his own weight. The guidance counselor dug around in his desk until he found a blank piece of paper and a ballpoint pen that still had some ink, then scratched his e-mail address onto the paper and slid it across the desk to Brad, never quite looking at him.

"Cool," said Brad, bobbing his head with feverish nonchalance, as if he regularly made plans to hang out with new acquaintances. He slid the scrap of paper into his pocket, pushing it down deep so as to be sure not to lose it. "Um." Glancing at the clock on Duane's tablet, he saw that they were just about to hit the exact ten-minute mark; nodding at it by way of explanation, he slowly stood. He nearly said *Saved by the bell*, with a little forced laugh, and caught himself at the last second, horrified. What a stupid thing to say that would have been! It totally would have come across like an insult! Even if he only would have been referring to the creepy strange intensity of this encounter, following this script that neither guy had had a chance to rehearse.

Anyway. He hadn't said it.

"All right," said Duane, with a nod. "I look forward to hearing from you."

All afternoon and all night Brad agonized over how soon he should write, and what he should say. Katie's whole future could ride on whether Duane helped them. Keith's, too. But Katie was the gifted one. She was the one who could lift her brother up along with her.

If he wrote too soon he'd look desperate; too late, he'd look like he didn't care. He managed to hold out till the next day. Dropping the kids off in the morning, he couldn't even look at the school without getting short of breath. The guidance counselor was somewhere inside there right now! It felt like it would be disastrous if he and Duane ran into each other before Brad sent the e-mail. Like, then it would be too late. He would have missed his chance to mold the parameters of their relationship.

From the school he went straight to the v-brothel where he had sex with a man via a male sexbot. When he got home he decided it was time to write the e-mail.

He did. Then he checked his tablet compulsively every three minutes to see if Duane had written back, convinced he wasn't going to.

But he did. He wanted to know where they would meet.

Brad, after too much thought, suggested Zack's, a sports bar not far from his apartment, close enough that the taxi fare wouldn't be too high. Or, if he'd had a slow week and opted to spare the expense of a taxi, it wouldn't be too far to drive, in case he got tipsy.

He suggested Tuesday, because his sister-in-law Ellen was already planning to come over that night anyway. God knew who he'd get to watch the kids if Duane requested a different night—springing for a babysitter would hurt. He sent Ellen a quick text, saying, "Hey, gr8 that u coming Tues night! Esp. since turns out i have sthing i really really nned 2 do that night. U dont mind watching kids, do u? Thanx!"

After he sent the text he quickly logged out of all his accounts and shut down his tablet—he didn't relish getting Ellen's reply.

Turning off the tablet felt weird. Everything seemed too bright and loud in the sudden silence. Then the noises from Katie's and Keith's tablets asserted themselves from behind their bedroom door, and the rumbling-bass music from the cars passing outside forced its vibrations into his flesh.

Four

Brad had a second fuck-session with Duane before their hang-out. Suiting up, it was slightly weird to think about being in the brothel with the guy, knowing that soon they'd be together in the everyday world, in Zack's. His Becky persona took over once the session started, though, and the weirdness went away.

Brad was not a *prostitute*. Prostitution was, of course, illegal. On the other hand, virtual-brothels "staffed" by perfectly realistic simulacra of human bodies—sexbots—were perfectly legal. Partly thanks to big-tech lobbying, but also thanks to the fact that a sexbot was not a person and therefore could not be exploited, as a person could be.

Lots of folks just visited v-brothels to have sex with an uninhabited sexbot, controlled by an AI. (You could also buy your own sexbot and keep it at home, but it would cost about three times as much as a car and could be embarrassing if found by, say, a guest, or your kid.) Sex with an AI *ought* to be perfectly satisfying. Computers took charge of activities much more complicated than fucking, all the time.

But for some not-yet-unquantified reason, an uninhabited sexbot was never quite convincing. And corporations like Kauffman-Berlini had discovered that some people would pay more—a lot more—to have sex with a sexbot operated by a human. Enough to justify the expense of setting up v-brothel chambers with bleeding-edge VR tech for contractors like Brad who showed up there to do their brotheling remotely.

The Neo-Christian League might have managed to get proxy brotheling classed as prostitution, if they hadn't been up against big tech lobbying. But Brad would have argued that such a classification would have been nonsense. Because who was being exploited? True, the clients paid extra for the intangible but real something that a real human presence brought to the fucking. But it was the real human presence of a person who didn't exist.

Ellen did let him know what she thought about him slipping out on her family visit, but subtly; she wouldn't say anything too direct about it with the kids present. Brad withered under the hot waves of her disapproval. Still, he'd known Ellen wouldn't leave him hanging, even if she might bitch. He didn't know why she'd want him there, anyway. He could understand her wanting to see the kids because they were blood relations, but she and Brad had never been close. Hell, Brad hadn't even been close with his own wife.

He'd leaned toward taking a taxi, since he'd be drinking. But he'd been low on johns the last few days, and when you factored in the cost of two or three beers he wasn't sure he could afford the fare. When Brad had been a little kid and auto-cabs had been about to appear, people had said they would be really cheap, because there was no driver who needed to be paid. But automobile lobbyists had gotten a big tax added to auto-cab fares.

His wipers screeched as they sloshed the rain back and forth across his windshield. Probably needed to be replaced.

As he turned into the strip-mall's parking lot the car slid a little and he cried out. Not in fear, but frustration. He'd have to figure out how to replace the worn tires. Couldn't keep driving around like this with the kids in the car.

He parked. The stumpy little strip mall contained a communal gaming center, a Robomat restaurant, a shuttered clothing store, and the bar. The bulk of the cars were clumped around Zack's. Brad checked to see if he was trembling; didn't seem to be. What if Duane stood him up?... Well, in that case he'd just sit there and drink a beer alone and get up and leave like that had been his plan all along. No one would have to know about his failure. Would just be a waste of money, was all.

He went inside. Duane was there, waiting.

Brad saw him right away, in spite of everything. "Everything" being the dim, yellowish lighting; the haze of water vapor from people's vaping; the clumps of roaring, guffawing males, sometimes with a female or two at their centers, grouped around the dart boards, pool tables, and the skeeball games along the wall. Most everybody here had come with a big group, their barking roars punching holes through the thick morass of the pounding rock soundtrack, crackling out of the fuzzy speakers.

Duane's unassuming meekness served as a beacon, in this sea of mostly-masculine assertion and hooting; he was sitting on a stool at the bar, fingers tapping his hardly-touched pint glass, an empty stool beside him. Duane noticed Brad right away, as well. From the relief on his face, Brad could tell that Duane had been dreading having to explain to someone that they couldn't sit on the stool because he was saving it, and dreading the humiliation if he got stood up after having explained that he was waiting for someone.

Duane grimaced, raised his eyebrows, raised his glass towards the empty stool in invitation. Brad grimaced back, nodded as he crossed the room. Neither wanted to acknowledge being happy the other had come, or being nervous, or anything like that, because then it would really start to feel like some sort of gay thing.

Sliding onto the stool, Brad said, "Hey. Thanks for coming."

"My pleasure."

Not that they really "said" these things—they shouted them, so as to be heard over the music and the ambient commotion. Verbal communication necessitated ducking their heads intimately close to each other.

"Anyway," began Brad, then came to halt. Maybe it would be weird and rude to leap right in and talk about the Pence Academy. To buy time, he made eye contact with Duane and then glanced apologetically in the bartender's direction, thus signaling to Duane that he'd be ready to start talking once he got his beer. Duane nodded and leaned his head back out of the cone of audibility.

Both of them sat wordlessly until Brad had managed to get his beer ordered and his debit card in the bartender's hand. During the silence they kept in touch, so to speak, with embarrassed glances, polite smiles, eye-rolls over how slow the service was. Once he had the beer ordered, before it had arrived, Brad leaned back into the cone. Duane followed suit. Brad said, "Okay. So where were we?"

"What do you mean?" asked Duane, afraid he'd missed a cue, or misheard over all the noise.

"No, I only meant, you know, what's up, how are you. I just don't want to be rude, you know. By talking about my stuff first thing. I just wanted to see how you, you know, I mean, I don't want to dominate, is all."

"Oh, I don't think you're dominating."

"Okay. Well, let's, uh, let's hang out."

Duane nodded, accepting this challenge to "hang out." Apparently his notion of hanging out was to get down to business. "I did manage to look at Katie's files."

"Finally got the tablet working, huh?" joked Brad. He was scared to talk about Katie's scores. If the news were bad, that would be it. It would be hard to get Duane to go back and contradict himself, once he'd already expressed an opinion.

"Actually, I had to borrow another faculty member's." Both men shook their heads with rueful grins, trying to forge a bit of camaraderie.

Duane continued: "Anyway, I did get a chance to look at Katie's scores. The full dossier. And it's true, she is above average."

In Duane's apologetic, hesitant, guilty tone was an approaching "but." To head it off, Brad blurted, "She is, she really is. Especially when you consider a lot of the stuff she's been through."

"Oh?" Duane's interest was piqued. The Pence Academy sometimes took mitigating factors into account, when a student's test scores weren't quite stellar—anyway, according to the rumors Brad had read online, they did. And it made sense that they would, because the Pence Academy wasn't truly an elite school, it was just better than the public ones. Its status wasn't so high that it couldn't afford to be merciful. If Brad could provide such a mitigating factor, he felt sure Duane would do his best to use it to help Katie. Because Duane was a nice guy. Brad had seen that, in the brothel.

"Yeah. Well. For example, her mom. Her mom died."

"Oh." Duane's face clouded. "Yes, I did see that in the file, too."

Brad could interpret this cloud. It meant Duane felt guilty for not having thought to give his condolences for Megan's death. "It was nearly a year ago," said Brad, and took his biggest gulp yet of beer. He'd been sad when she'd died, but in some ways it had been a relief. Even economically, it had turned out for the best. Because as long as she'd been alive it never would have even occurred to him to audition to become a brotheler. He signaled the bartender for a refill. Fuck the tab. He felt frustrated. There was a simple task that he ought to be able to do, but instead he couldn't even figure out exactly what it was. "Let's hang out," he repeated, with insistence. "So, tell me about you. What's it like, being a guidance counselor? How'd you start?"

Duane shrugged. "It's, you know. I'm lucky to have it. I originally planned to be a teacher. Lots more slots, you know. More jobs, better odds. But then, when I was about to go into my junior year of college and pick my specialization, the government decided they needed guidance counselors. Because no one had wanted to become one for the past, like, twenty years. So they offered a pretty substantial subsidy on a degree in that field. And I'd run out of money at the end of my sophomore year and had had to take two years off, trying to save up enough to go back. Working as a monitor of web content aggregation programs, which frankly sucked. So I took the subsidy and enrolled in the guidance counselor track."

"A big subsidy?"

"Well. Not that big. But I needed whatever they would give me. And the repayment terms were pretty good—almost twenty years, at very low interest. A heck of a lot lower than my student loans. I'll be buried with my student loan debts. But that subsidy, I should have it finally paid back sometime next year."

This was awesome, Brad thought—they were really talking. Duane even started to seem hoarse. Brad even almost forgot about Katie, he was having so much fun. "And, I mean, it's worked out. You've got a great job." Hurriedly he added, "I mean, I'm sure sometimes it gets aggravating for *you*. I just meant, you're a success, is all."

Duane shrugged again and sipped his beer. "It's a good job. But the programs have changed. When they offered that subsidy, obviously, the idea was that they would need lots more guidance counselors. But then not too long after I got the job the EdDep policy changed and our role was downgraded. I mean, obviously I still feel super-lucky and grateful. But there's all this consolidation now. Our school is a combination of what used to be eight different schools, with eight different guidance counselors. Now there's only me."

Brad nodded. When it had come time to enroll Katie in kindergarten, he'd been shocked by how big the campus had been. Now, of course, it was much bigger. The consolidations had started sometime between when he'd graduated and when his daughter had turned five; it must have been in some of the newsfeeds, he supposed.

He said, "That's what I mean, though. You're a success. Out of those eight people, they picked you to stay. You must be the best."

"Luck of the draw, mostly. The next time they consolidate, I might be out."

At the thought that the school might be consolidated yet again while his kids were still there, burying them yet deeper in anonymous riff-raff, Brad got that familiar drowning feeling. "You've done good stuff, though. You've made a difference. Helped kids. I'm sure of it."

"Oh, I don't know." Duane seemed to understand that this was an invitation to turn the conversation back around to Brad's children, and to do it in a roundabout way, that would allow him to hold off on announcing his judgment of her scores, and chances. "It must have been hard for Katie and Keith. Losing their mother."

"Well. Sure." Brad was halfway done with his second beer. He could already feel the alcohol's loosening effect; it had been a long while since he'd drunk regularly, and his tolerance had gone way down. "It was a confusing time for them in general. See, Megan and I had sorta split up. And we were kind of passing the kids back and forth. Then we sorta worked it out, and had decided to get back together. And that's when she died in the car wreck."

"Oh my God," said Duane, aghast. "That's awful. I'm so sorry."

Brad nodded, accepting his condolences, avoiding eye contact. Frustrated; he would have liked to explain to Duane that he had actually been, well, sad, but also relieved. Life with Megan was going to be hell, worse even than the first go-round. They were only going to get back together for the sake of the kids; partly for the whole nuclear-family thing, but mainly so as to pool their financial resources. Her getting killed in the car wreck gave him an out that he didn't have to blame himself for. If only he could have, like, three more beers, he would be able to explain all that; if Duane had the same amount, he'd be juiced enough to listen, instead of stopping Brad before he said anything too personal. Fuck the money, even, Brad would actually be willing to spend the money. But how would he manage to drive home? How would he pay the parking toll if he had to take a cab and leave his car here at Zack's overnight? Plus if the taxi's AI figured out he was drunk then the fare would be higher, because his need would be greater.... It sucked that here they were, taking this drug that would actually allow them to talk about their feelings; but they couldn't take enough of it to *really* talk about them, because then they wouldn't be able to drive home.

It was still too early to come out and beg for Duane's help with Katie. Brad knew that his plea would be most effective if he could make friends with Duane first.

Besides, making his spiel prematurely would bring the conversation to its end, *before* he'd had a chance to befriend Duane. It had been years since he'd hung out with someone for no good reason. Tonight he did indeed have a good reason; but the longer he put off thinking about it, the longer he could pretend that he didn't, that they were just hanging out.

Looking for a way to orient the conversation around Katie while still beating around the bush, he said, "I try to look for ways to stimulate the kids. Culturally, intellectually, stuff like that. It's hard to find the time, though."

"Yeah. What do you do for work?"

"Customer-service stuff. I work remotely. But anyway, the reason I mentioned that was, maybe you have recommendations? Of stuff like that to do? I just thought, you know, because of your profession and your training and all."

"Oh, you know. I mean, '*training*.' It's not much to speak of." Once those words had left his mouth Duane tensed his mouth muscles, as if to physically stop himself from saying more. Maybe he feared his disparagement of his own credentials would leak back to the EdDep managers who controlled his fate. Or maybe he feared making Brad lose confidence in him. "But, ah. I don't know. I mean, there are lots of resources. Like, the Meerville Arts Center."

"Oh, I've been there." True, strictly speaking. Not since a school trip over twenty years ago, though.

Duane lit up. "Oh, really? You go there often?"

"Not as often as I'd like." Hurriedly, trying to head off any traps, he said, "I mean, I don't *know* anything about art."

"Oh, me neither. Not really. But I do go there sometimes."

"How did you get into art?"

Flustered, Duane said, "I wouldn't say I'm *into* it," hastily disowning any claim to expertise. "But it's just, I don't know, I sometimes feel sort of drawn to it." He winced to hear his own pompous language. "Just, I like looking at the old stuff. From other, I don't know. Other times."

"What, um, uh … what's that mean?"

"Oh. Um. I don't know. Just, like, my, whatever. Feeling."

"But so you think I should take Katie and Keith to the Arts Center?"

"Well ... I don't know. Now that I think about it, maybe it's a little quiet for kids. Might be beyond their attention spans."

Brad's first instinct was to get defensive and insist that Katie would be perfectly capable of walking through an art museum. But he kept quiet because he knew that was bullshit. Keith might be able to behave himself in such a place—he was the quieter one. Less high-energy. But Katie was the gifted one, the one who might pull herself and her brother up out of the universal quicksand, so she was the one he needed to think of.

He said, "Maybe I should go to the Arts Center myself first, then. Check it out. See if maybe it would be suitable for the kids." He didn't know why he said that. Instinct, maybe.

A long moment of silence followed from Duane. Brad almost feared he'd offended the guy. But no—Duane was just chewing on something, debating whether to say it.

At last he did. "Well, maybe I could show you around sometime. If you like. Just because, I mean, I'm not an *expert*, but I do know it sort of well, now."

Pleasure warmed Brad's body. "Sure, man. Sure, sure. That'd be really cool."

Five

Wednesday, while the kids were at school, Brad had a fuck-session in the guise of a man, having sex with another man. He thought he'd done a pretty good job, handling the john's body expertly, timing everything so as to bring him to a massive orgasm only minutes before the end of the session. Good bang for the buck, so to speak. His head wasn't as tightly in the game as he thought, though; he didn't even take proper note of the client's silence as they dressed, until the guy scowled tearfully and said, "You barely even *talked* to me!"

Brad's mouth fell open, then he stammered an apology as the john stamped out of his brothel room, melting out of Brad's VR reality. There went that positive rating. But what hit him harder was that he had been professionally remiss. Part of the reason people paid extra to fuck an android being controlled by a real, live person was that they wanted to talk, without the pressure of having to face someone's real, physical body and "real" persona. (Others, of course, paid for the satisfaction of knowing they were telling a real person, and not just a robot, to shut his or her fucking mouth.) It had been unconscionable for Brad to ignore this basic need.

He'd found a blog claiming that another wave of school consolidations was coming, and that when it ended there would only be four or five public schools in the whole state. Dwelling on what classroom conditions would be like afterward was distracting him from his work. Whenever they did a consolidation they mashed all the students together, but never brought along all the teachers. Katie would wind up in a class with at least three hundred kids. He had to get her into the Pence Academy before that happened.

The worries that distracted him from his other clients fed into his session with Duane and made him more attentive. Not that he tried to worm his exterior life's concerns into their fuck-sessions, not directly. But he'd been doing a lot of thinking about Duane these days, and it led in a natural way to an amped-up interest in the guy, which translated into an elevated sensitivity toward him, and a greater ability to pick up on his desires, non-sexual ones but sexual ones too.

This was their fourth session together—that was a lot, in a very short time, but it felt like they'd had even more. And in the external world, in just a couple of days, they were actually going to go to the Arts Center together.

They had a little chat as they were undressing (this time Duane had remained dressed until the sexbot activated, in order to have the erotic experience of Brad undressing him; in his preference box he'd requested that the sexbot be clad in complicated lingerie, the dismantling of which plainly gave him a certain *frisson*). Both of them kinda-sorta wanted to keep talking a while instead of leaping right into things, and each sensed that desire in the other; Brad laughed about it as he pulled gently on Duane's penis. Duane laughed too, as he took Brad's sexbot avatar in his arms. They each knew why the other was laughing, and that they were both laughing for the same reasons, even though neither of them had said anything.

Ankles up by his ears and mouth full of the flapping wet rubber paddle that aped the motion of Duane's tongue, in some other neighborhood of Meerville, Brad wondered why that was? It must be because a friendship had sprung up between them.

Once they were panting on the slab, post-coital, Brad said, "Did you bring your vape?"

Duane laughed. "It's in my bag," he admitted. "But don't worry, I'm not going to vape. Like I told you, I only wanted to do it because they do it in movies."

"I was going to ask if *I* could borrow it."

Duane stared at Brad, startled, as if the sexbot body might have turned into a real girl, Pinnochio-like. "What? But why?

I mean … I mean, your lungs aren't connected to the android's lungs. They're miles away. Why would you want to vape?"

"Because I want to do like they do in the old movies." That was true, even though he'd never heard of these movies before Duane.

Duane laughed, and rolled off the slab to retrieve his bag. He checked the fluid levels of the vape-stick, then paused with his thumb on the power switch as his eyes went to the wall-mounted digital clock. Brad moved his own head to direct the VR avatar's gaze; in the far-off room with Duane, the sexbot's head aped his motion, and its android eyes registered the sight of the clock and transmitted it back to Brad in his suit. Not that he needed it; he had his own timer in the lower left quadrant of his vision.

"I guess we shouldn't," said Duane. "Time's almost up."

"That's okay. I can stick around."

"Really? It's no problem?"

"Sure." Brad had no more sessions today. Duane was his third—he'd planned on going home to lie down for an hour before picking up the kids, but he could hang out instead. Duane was a client he hoped to cultivate, after all, even regardless of the stuff with the Pence Academy. As for his employers, when he'd been hired the video tutorials had explained to Brad that he did have a certain latitude in staying late, as long as it didn't interfere with an upcoming session and as long as the sexbot operator didn't fuck free of charge.

However, off-the-clock fraternizing could go too far. If management decided the contractor had crossed the line, they reserved the right to take action, up to and including termination of contract. Since the location of that line was entirely at management's discretion, Brad would have to be cautious not to abuse the privilege.

Right now, though, he felt like hanging out. Just for today.

They sat cross-legged on the slab, passing the vape-stick back and forth, grinning, almost giggly. They hardly even noticed being naked.

"So," said Brad. "You wanted to vape because in old movies that's what they do after sex. You like old movies?"

"Oh, sure. Movies now are just flashing lights and screaming, but back in the day they had more story. Like, I know they're silly, but I like those old *Fast and Furious* movies. Have you heard of them?"

"I *think* so," lied Brad, scrunching up his face in concentration.

"You should check them out sometime.... I mean," he hurriedly added, in sudden fear of judgment, "they're not great art or anything. But what I like about them is that in every movie, there's a goal they have to reach, and they go through steps to reach it. And each character is really well-defined. They each have their own look, and their own strengths and weaknesses, and each one interacts with the rest of the group in a particular way."

Brad nodded sagely, taking a hit off the stick. "Yeah, movies nowadays don't know how to do that. You can never tell what's supposed to be going on."

"Sometimes there really isn't anything that's supposed to be going on. The visuals are better now, of course."

Brad nodded again. They passed the stick back and forth a couple times. Duane wasn't even looking at Brad's tits. It was as if they were an affectionate old married couple, who had seen each other naked a billion times before.

Brad took another drag, hesitating before speaking, trying to gauge how much of a bleed-through he could risk between this world and the mundane one. Back in his real body, away from the sexbot, the pressure pads in the suit mimicked the feel of the pipe in his fingers and on his lips, and the wires connecting his hand to the floor mimicked its infinitesimal weight with the gentlest of distributed tugs; he breathed in plain old air and held it in his lungs, then expelled it; some part of his brain had been assigned the task of hypnotizing himself into experiencing the effects of the nicotine. In a casual tone that betrayed no hint of how long he'd mulled over whether to ask the question, he said, "You mentioned great art. Do you like art?"

"I do, actually. Do you?"

"I don't know anything about it. I always wanted to learn."

"Oh, well, I don't *know* anything about it. I just like looking at it, is all."

It would be too similar to their conversation at Zack's if Brad mentioned the Meerville Arts Center. He thought of asking if Duane owned any art, but that risked sounding like he was feeling out Duane's level of personal wealth. He tried, "How did you get into art? How did you find out about it?"

"Well, I always *knew* about art. Like, that it existed."

"Yeah, but you know what I mean."

"I just, um." He laughed, and peeked nervously up at Brad from the vape-stick. "I can tell you … I mean, this relationship, I mean I know we don't have a *relationship* so don't worry, but I mean this, sort of, arrangement, it's different from a normal social situation. Right? So I feel like I can, you know, say things to you. That I wouldn't under normal circumstances. If that's all right."

"You can say whatever you want to me."

"Okay. Well, what I was going to say before that big long digression was just, I get lonely. There. I mean, obviously I'm not married or anything. Or, well, I guess sometimes people, uh…."

Brad nodded confirmation. "Lots of married people do come here. I guess they figure it's not cheating, because the sexbot isn't literally a person." He didn't mention the couples who came in seeking the threesome option; he didn't want Duane's head going there. Normally he avoided reminding a john that the sexbot was a mere android. It felt like he and Duane had reached a point where they could dispense with a lot of the bullshit, though. Reaching over to take the vape-stick, Brad patted Duane's arm and said, "I didn't figure you for someone who was sneaking over here behind his wife's back, though."

As compliments go, it was pretty tame. Made Duane smile and duck his head, though.

"Anyway," he continued. "I used to want to go out and be around people. Someplace other than the street. Bars were too expensive, and I never met anyone there, and even if I had the music would be too loud to get to know them. So one day I tried the museum, just because the ticket price is pretty low, at least."

"And there were people there?"

"Uh. Yeah. But that's the thing, I kind of lost interest in them. Because the art was so interesting. Now, when I go there, I usually look for spots where there *aren't* many people."

Brad sensed it as Duane considered and then rejected saying other stuff, too. That was okay. Brad would have the opportunity to investigate further when he and Duane actually went to the Arts Center together, out in the other world.

Six

Duane led the way through the lobby of the Meersville Arts Center, yammering to Brad about how he didn't really know that much about the place in an effort to disavow the silly pleasure of guiding someone new into this thing he liked. As they negotiated the shouting crowd, Brad felt like he ought to say something to show interest. So he asked what kind of stuff they had here, anyway. Just, like, paintings and things? Like, on the walls?

The Center had front-loaded all the famous stuff, Duane explained. Towards the back of the museum the rooms got less crowded. As they stood in the ticket line Brad called up the Arts Center's map on his tablet and saw that the Instagram Tour, a bright line snaking through the galleries that flashed in alternating green, yellow, blue and red on his screen, was concentrated in the front half of the building.

The banners and poster-screens festooning the lobby consumed the eye. Gradually, though, Brad noticed that the cheerful voices blaring from multiple directions about today's exhibitions, and the newest additions to the Center's suite of apps, had a funny echo to them; peering more closely, he realized that the poster-screens and banners pressing in all around disguised how large the space really was.

Brad's reaction must have been more pronounced than he'd thought; "Yeah, it's pretty grand, actually," said Duane, making him jump. Brad closed his mouth and lowered his gaze back to Duane's level, who continued: "If you think about it, I mean. Imagine it without all the people here."

It *was* grand. The ceiling was way, way high, higher even than the skylight of the mall. It was made of gray stone cut into rounded, concave shapes.

More people filled the space than Brad would have expected. Of course, many of the loudest folks worked for the museum, barkers in blinking multicolored neckties roaming the lobby, shouting to the patrons shuffling through the line about the hottest painting, the latest exhibits, and the benefits of membership.

"They brought in a new marketing firm last year," said Duane. "I think it's worked out really well for them."

Duane had said that he could get them a discount with his school district ID. But the AI running the ticket kiosk seemed unimpressed, no matter how many times he scanned his ID card, and the human employee he hailed just looked mildly scandalized that he would angle for a discount. Grumblings in the line behind them grew audible. Embarrassed, Duane had to ask for a few more dollars from Brad, who'd only given him enough to cover an admission ticket *with* the discount. With a few taps on his tablet screen Brad transferred the extra money over from his account to Duane's.

Once finished at the kiosk, they wended their way through the crowd to one of the narrow entry points. They patiently let themselves be pushed along through the entry by the press of people. Theoretically the cameras mounted all along the doorway should be able to read their tickets' barcodes automatically, as long as they held them with the barcodes exposed. But as Brad and Duane passed through, the red light flashed and a klaxon went off. Those who'd gone through the gate at about the same time as Brad and Duane, their fellow possible culprits, sailed on into the museum. Brad and Duane dutifully waited, till a sullen, sleepy security guy shuffled over to check their tickets. He seemed to have zero interest in tracking down whoever had snuck in, or had palmed off a bum ticket. Maybe the automated ticket-taker screwed up all the time, and the security guy knew it.

The first room was filled with big statues of naked people, made from white rock. On the lap of a statue of a nude woman

46

combing her hair, a thirty-something woman had climbed; she perched there, flashing the Victory sign and sticking out her tongue, as her friend shrieked and snapped a photo. "Are these, like, Greek statues?" asked Brad.

"French, mainly. Three, four hundred years old. This room is a big stop on the Instagram Tour. But let's head to the back, there's cool stuff back there."

Duane took Brad and showed him his hide-outs. Rooms that sometimes literally had no one else in them; when other people *were* there, they held their tablets to their ears, listening to the recorded tour guide chatter. Galleries with glass cases of Chinese lacquer-ware. A room of limestone statues from an island called Cyprus. The Signac room.

That first day, Brad took out his tablet and started to call up the Arts Center's site, in order to play the recorded tours on the app. Duane said, "The tour doesn't say anything that isn't already printed on the little info cards." Brad looked; indeed, beside each object was a little card giving a basic description of it. Duane continued: "Sometimes it's sort of neat not to listen to the description right away. To just kind of look at it."

It wasn't exactly a direct request for Brad not to play the recording. But Brad knew Duane hated to make direct requests, for anything. He put the tablet back in his pocket.

They stood over a glass case, looking down at a big red plate. Lacquer, whatever that was. Chinese. The thing was more than a foot in diameter. A dizzying fistful of squirming, undifferentiated detail tried to cram itself into Brad's mind; he blinked appreciatively, and prepared to move down the line to the next piece.

"I like this one," said Duane, referring to the big red plate. "Every time you look at it, you see more stuff."

"You've looked at this same plate more than once?" asked Brad, surprised.

"Sure," said Duane, once again self-conscious. "I told you. I come here a lot."

Somehow it hadn't sunk in that Duane came and looked at the same things over and over. Brad looked again at the big red plate. He felt a little silly, staring at something that wasn't going to move, that didn't have a display that could change.

He was surprised to see frolicking children resolve themselves out of that mass of detail. Chubby children with weird haircuts; their heads shaved nearly bald, except for sprouting forelocks. They wore robes decorated in floral patterns. The kids were gamboling around in a big room … uh, no, actually, as he kept looking he realized that there weren't any walls. Or maybe there were walls, just covered with wallpaper depicting nature scenes … except did they even have wallpaper back in old-timey China?… Anyway, he was pretty sure it was actual nature, rivers and hills and mountains and clouds and stuff. So they must be out running around on some sort of patio. More kids popped into existence out of the detailed monochrome as he stared, despite the fact that the plate wasn't doing anything; ladies, too, in big complicated dresses and with alarmingly deformed eyebrows; also plants in big pots. Houseplants, he supposed. Except they weren't in the house, they were out on the patio. Or in a gazebo. He counted the kids and ladies, as a way of fixing them in place, his eyes hunting and pecking through the clumps of detail. Along the way he kept finding other things rising out of the complex pattern of the patio floor, which was completely regular but had at first appeared to him a squirmy wormy chaotic jumble. He realized that speckled all over the patio were these, like, peculiarly-shaped rocks, although he had no idea what they were doing there. Maybe they were decorative? Did people decorate with just plain rocks? They were interesting-shaped, so maybe. In old times, no doubt they'd done stuff differently.

"You're right," said Brad, taken aback, as if Duane had introduced him to an exotic, clever form of optical illusion. Almost every image that had ever been presented to him had been designed to be entirely taken in and understood within seconds, at the longest. The experience of letting his eyes sink into depths of detail, of looking at an image that, Brad began to suspect, might be designed for *hours* of study, had a perverse luxury to it, and began to make Brad feel almost drunk. It was a goofy pleasure, and he was glad there were no strangers in the room to catch him at it. But he understood how Duane had gotten hooked, and was grateful to him for having introduced the phenomenon.

They met there pretty regularly. Duane's schedule required him to be at work from seven till eleven in the morning, then after a five-hour break to return at four and stay at the office till nine. Brad sometimes got too booked to meet him during that five-hour window. Which was good, because he needed the money. Still, he couldn't help but be glad when his schedule allowed him to meet Duane at the Arts Center. Of course, sometimes, when he was too booked for the Center, part of the reason was that Duane himself had made an appointment at the brothel. But having a fuck-session via the sexbot was not the same as being just a couple of guys hanging out.

The brothel's lunch rush was how Brad made most of his money. On days when he was too booked to meet Duane at the Arts Center, he wished he could sometimes fuck in the evenings instead. But the desire made him feel guilty, because the evening was when he spent time with Keith and Katie.

Turned out Duane was right that it was more fun to explore the neglected back of the museum, away from the Instagram Tour, where they stored the stuff less suited to being the backdrop for a photo. For example, the Signac room, untouched by the Tour: actually three small rooms, opening one onto the other; black walls and dozens of watercolors under glass, by some French guy named Paul Signac from the 1800's. Most of the paintings were of boats, but not all. To enter the rooms one passed through a glass door with Paul Signac's signature stamped on the glass; it was in cursive, which the schools had stopped teaching long before Brad's time, but if he stared long enough he could make out the letters. Duane and Brad agreed that this guy must have been famous, to get a whole room to himself, yet they'd never heard of him.

"I guess he's even more famous than Picasso?" said Brad, once. Picasso was one of the few painters he'd ever heard of, before he'd started coming to the museum; they never went to look at his paintings, because they were always mobbed by the Instagram Tour. "I mean, they gave Paul Signac these rooms all to himself. They don't give Picasso whole rooms."

Duane nodded. But he said, "Or maybe Signac is less famous than Picasso, and that's why they can afford a whole room's worth of his paintings."

That was pretty smart, Brad thought. Duane was always doing that, saying something pretty smart.

Almost from the beginning, neither of them was shy about their own ignorance, not in front of each other. Their ignorance was exciting; the greater its extent, the bigger the world that awaited their exploration.

Not infrequently, one or both of them would regard some object and feel an aesthetic thrill. But for the most part their experiences were aspirational. Anyone could see that lots of trouble had been taken to create these things—in fact, Brad gradually began to realize that, in many cases, lots and lots and *lots* of trouble had been taken. He started to suspect that more trouble had been taken with, say, the larger and more complex pieces of Chinese lacquer ware, than any single person had ever taken with any one object or video or process Brad had experienced in his entire life. They must have had a reason. In their culture, it must have been plain to see why a chunk of lacquer would be worth such trouble. Of course, Brad and Duane had access to plenty of words that purported to account for such phenomena: "self-expression," "beauty," and so forth. But none of these terms had enough oomph in them to actually explain anything; one felt embarrassed if one said them aloud. Whatever system of values had produced most of these objects was largely opaque to Brad. Yet such a system clearly had existed—the pieces were here to prove it. Just the fact that it had existed, that it therefore did still exist in the realm of the possible, excited him. Even if he personally harbored little hope of deciphering that system for himself.

When they hung out at the Arts Center, Duane would give Brad updates on his efforts to steer Katie into the Pence Academy. That he did so without prompting, without Brad having to broach the subject, warmed him towards the guidance counselor still more; it bled into the fuck-sessions, making him yet more attentive and solicitous.

"So you think it's really going to work out?" said Brad, one day. They were back at the lacquer room. This was to be a short museum visit; Brad had only a two-and-a-half-hour window, having been a female in a lesbian tryst at eleven and scheduled to be back at the mall before four in order to be a female for the sake of two fifty-something guys.

"No promises, of course," said Duane. "But I am allowed to send a certain number of names out, with my recommendations. I can't just pick whoever I want; the test rankings do most of the deciding. But Katie's scores squeak her into the running, as long as I add a letter explaining that her in-person comportment makes up for any lack in her rankings."

Duane turned a worried eye Brad's way. "You know ... we probably shouldn't mention to anyone that we do this. See each other, socially. Not till after Katie's application to the Pence Academy has been evaluated. And, well, even then. It could make people suspicious of my motives in recommending her, if they found out that we were ... uh, well ... you know." He ended the sentence with one of his blushes.

Brad knew that the word Duane had gotten stuck on was "friends." He nodded, fighting off his own blush. There was something humiliating about being in a relationship with no obvious value, no transactional element. That was the kind of thing kids did, not grown men. Weirdly, the one thing more humiliating than to be in this relationship whose only value was squishy kid-shit like "feelings" and "emotional needs" was the memory, constantly recurring, that it was *not* like that. He absolutely was here because he needed something from Duane; he needed that shot at the Pence Academy for Katie.

He nursed hopes that this friendship would extend on into some future in which its utilitarian origins would have become obsolete; Katie would be safely ensconced in the Pence Academy, which would later give her at least a chance to participate in the coming Jobs Renaissance that was forever being promised. Then he and Duane could continue to meet and hang out here at the Arts Center, and even though they would never talk about it they would both see that it was clearly for no good reason that they were hanging out, and if it was for no good reason then the reason must be that they were friends. (Presumably Duane would also continue booking fuck-sessions with Brad at the v-brothel. But that was a whole separate sphere of existence, with no relation to the social situation Brad was daydreaming about now, and with only a limited relation to the social entity called "Brad" who visited the museum with Duane.)

Keeping his face as clear as possible of all his conflicting emotions and shame, Brad nodded. "I'll be discreet," he promised.

"Thanks. For Katie's sake, but also … well, it could look bad, for me, if people thought I was showing favoritism. There's no rules against socializing with parents of students. But they could still fire me for it, if they wanted."

"Don't worry. But are we still on for the baseball game?"

"Oh, sure. It's not like we're going to bump into anyone who'd know who we are." Nobody ever bumped into anyone in Meerville.

Baseball was what Brad had decided to bring to the table, in exchange for Duane's gift of art. As a little boy his dad had sometimes taken him to see the Meerville Meteors, and before he'd had kids Brad had sometimes watched their games online. Lately he'd started entering the raffle for free tickets; he might even spring to just buy a couple.

They were in the Mesoamerican gallery now. Maybe part of the reason Brad had mentioned their baseball plans was that they were standing in front of a case containing a ceramic statuette of a grinning guy with a huge head and a very thick belt; the figure was labelled "Ball Player." Supposedly it had been made in, like, 900 C.E. Brad wasn't entirely sure, but he thought that was before Christopher Columbus had sailed to the United States. Before he'd started hanging out at the museum with Duane, he'd never even heard of such a place as "Mesoamerica." Now he could find it on a map. He took a secret, childish pleasure in the fact.

"But so," he said. "You really think you'll be able to get Katie into the Pence Academy? I know you can't promise it. But you really *think* so?" Brad knew he shouldn't press the point, shouldn't risk annoying the guy he was depending on for so much, but he couldn't restrain himself. Besides, he understood that even if Duane did get annoyed, that annoyance would not be enough to make him write Brad off, or screw Katie over out of spite. Although he had trouble letting himself believe it, although it made him nervous to be vulnerable to so much joy, he realized that he could trust Duane. Even though neither one of them could come out and say it, they really were friends. And in the look that Duane gave him now, Brad could see that Duane knew just what he was thinking, and that he himself felt the same way.

In general, Brad compartmentalized quite well, and there was not much seepage from his everyday "Brad" persona into his sexbot personae. Nevertheless, all those personae did share the same store of memories and knowledge, even if their impressions and reactions often differed. The next time Duane booked a fuck-session, the Brad that inhabited the sexbot remembered all that Duane had promised to do for Katie, and for a reward administered to the guidance counselor the blow job of his life. It was the type of experience that ruins one for lesser pleasures, and Duane surfaced from it blinking, disoriented, gaping into the sexbot's eyes with awe and a gratitude that bordered on fear.

Seven

Brad had filed a report on the initial mix-up with Duane, when Brad had found himself inhabiting a female instead of a male sexbot—he'd salvaged the situation that time, but the next could be a disaster. And it was.

Checking his dashboard, Brad saw that he had been booked to operate a male sexbot, in order to have a homosexual fuck-session with a male. Brad reported to the brothel, donned the suit, and let the VR reality melt him into the room, some unspecified distance away, where the male client awaited. So far, so good: the sexbot and the client were both male, as promised by the checklist on Brad's dashboard.

Only problem: the client had apparently not requested a male sexbot for a homosexual fuck-session.

As soon as the room melted into existence around Brad, he knew. The client was there, still fully dressed, fists bunched, face red, jaw tight, chest and shoulders heaving with fast, deep breaths. Brad took a step back before he'd gotten accustomed to the body, and nearly lost his balance and fell.

"The *fuck*?!" spat the client. It was supposed to be forceful, but his voice cracked. He was a weedy, red-headed guy, wearing jeans and the T-shirt of some corporation Brad had never heard of. "Huh? I said what the *fuck*, man?!"

"Oh, man," said Brad, holding up his hands with the palms out. "Don't tell me there's been a mix-up? If so, we'll totally give you a refund, sir." He refrained from asking why the client had waited for the sexbot to activate, instead of turning and walking out as soon as he'd seen its broad shoulders and big penis.

"A *refund*?!" the client shrieked, advancing on him. "A fucking *refund*?!"

"Uh, yeah, man," said Brad. He heard how high-pitched his voice had gotten, even emitted from the normally dark brown mellow tones of the masculine sexbot.

"How about an *apology*, faggot!" The client shoved Brad in the pectorals, knocking him off-balance and onto his back.

In his external life, for example out on the street, if someone had tried to push his physical body, Brad would have blocked the blow. Or at least tried to. Here in the brothel, though, he tended to be more passive. Partly thanks to the nature of the job. But also there should have been no need to defend himself because theoretically he would be yanked out of the simulation if things became violent.

So he expected, when he hit the floor, to find that he'd hit it in his own body, at his own v-brothel, back at the mall, pulled down by the wires attaching his suit to the walls and floor. Instead his insides flash-froze as he looked up to see the ginger client still advancing, and now actually trying to kick him. The kicks were aimed at his (or, rather, the sexbot's) penis; with a squeal Brad twisted out of the way, clapping hands over penis and testicles.

The ginger swung his foot out. The momentum nearly made him lose his balance and tumble over, himself—apparently the guy wasn't used to kicking people. He didn't aim the blow well, plus Brad twisted out of the way, so the kick glanced off Brad's hip. Naturally, the suit he wore was calibrated to transmit no harmful contact; the sexbot being beaten should no more leave Brad with bruises than it being butt-fucked should leave him with a stretched anus. Theoretically. Then again, theoretically the simulation should have shut off as soon as the violence started, so who knew what else might go haywire?

Not that Brad's fear followed from any chain of reasoning. Just the fact of someone bearing down on him, kicking at his nude body.

"Hatch!" he cried. That was the safe word, the escape hatch;

saying that word would instantly end the simulation. The video tutorials had assured him of this. "Hatch! Hatch! Hatch!"

Nothing changed. There was the guy. Drawing back his foot. *"Hatch!!"* screamed Brad.

Still expecting to get kicked in the privates, he melted back into his own suit-clad body, in the mall's hidden brothel, still screaming "Hatch!" For a few seconds he lay there, trembling, eyes darting, expecting to get kicked again.

By the time he sat up it was no longer fear that made his ears whine, but disgust and self-loathing that marinated his brain into a sickly, hangover-like headache.

Why had he bailed like that? The suit wouldn't have transmitted physically harmful pressure—it *wouldn't* have, he was certain. Even the sharpest blow would have been rendered as a tap by the pressure cushions.

There'd been no physical danger. Ergo, he should have ridden out the client's fit. Maybe physical violence was what the guy had really wanted all along. If what the client had wanted was to beat the crap out of him, letting it happen could have led to a positive review and maybe a repeat appointment.

The professional thing would have been to ride it out. Failing to do so was likely to cost him reviews and sessions; in other words, money. Cost him one more day provided for. One more day he could stave off financial ruin, one more day he wouldn't have to put his kids on half-days at school, or else pull them altogether, because he wouldn't be able to pay the textbook, lunch, and shuttling fees, and because he'd have to try to farm them out for work once they got old enough. Seriously, he should have indulged that client's fetish. Where was his head?

Eight

It was a rare Tuesday, in that Brad had no clients booked. It sucked not to be bringing in money. But also it was kind of nice; he and Duane had a date at the Arts Center, and Brad was glad to not have to make the effort of recalibrating his mind, glad to just be Brad all day so that he could be Brad more fully with his friend. Privately he had started using that word, "friend." He cherished the word, and to cherish something revealed to him his weakness, his vulnerability, his absurdity.

Duane and Brad had sprung for memberships—the outlay had made Brad wince. But they'd started coming often enough that it would save money in the long run. Even so, he had only been able to justify the expenditure by reminding himself that all this might end up getting Katie in the Pence Academy. Anyway, now they didn't have to line up at the ticket kiosks, they could just have their membership cards out in their hands when they left the lobby for the galleries and hope the AI spotted the barcodes. When they'd bought the membership, at an automated kiosk over in a corner of the lobby, they'd had to sit through an interminable tutorial on the special features of the Instagram Tour this membership gave them access to, as well as a long run-down of the Center's multiple apps. There had been no way to skip through all that and get to the pay screen, and it had eaten into a big chunk of their time at the museum.

Duane led the way to the Signac room. Brad could tell Duane had something to say that he was dreading. When he imagined what difficult thing Duane might have to say, all he came up with was an embarrassed, angry disquisition on how weird it was for two guys to be hanging out like this without any

59

reason at all. This possibility was so loud in Brad's brain that it drowned out any others.

As they maneuvered through the crowd of the Instagram Tour, Brad kept his mouth shut, cowed by his perception of Duane's displeasure. Then he realized this was exactly the wrong thing to do; if he didn't even talk, if he was just this ignorant lump of meat tagging along after Duane, expecting to have favors done for its kids and to be taught stuff about art, then no wonder Duane was getting tired of him. With forced cheer, he said, "So, hey, I think I got a few days picked out for those baseball tickets. Some Sunday games that I think I could be free on. I'll forward them to you, you'll let me know which one works best, and then I'll start figuring out a babysitter."

"Sure, that sounds great," said Duane, and in such an uncomplicated, straightforward way that for the first time Brad allowed himself to think something else might be bugging him.

They were clear of the tour's route now, passing through the room of statues from Cyprus. Sometimes the galleries not marked out for the tour were completely deserted, but today there was an intrepid couple who'd left the beaten track in search of fresh subjects for photos. The man had climbed onto the shoulders of an oversized statue of a king, and was licking its ear and leering at the camera, freezing in position and waiting for his mate to calm her hilarity enough to snap the photo. Once Brad and Duane had closed the door to the Signac room behind them, they could still hear the couple's whoops and hollering. But it wasn't too bad, and the distant cries and laughter of the Instagram Tour were even fainter.

Brad's remark had failed to spark a conversation about baseball. Almost solemnly, the two men stood before a watercolor of ships at harbor. To Brad, distracted, the sheet was a delirious blur of multicolored tesserae that he could only resolve into an image with effort. Beside him he could feel the dark twitching gravity of Duane's burden. He kept trying to tell himself that it was his imagination. Finally, though, the need to allay his anxiety and find out what was wrong outweighed his fear of looking ridiculous when it turned out to be nothing. Clearing his throat, he said, "Uh, hey, man. It seems like something's on your mind?"

Duane sighed. "Yeah, actually, there is," said Duane, with relief, but still reluctant to come out and say whatever it was.

"Something I did?"

Duane snapped his head towards him in surprise. "What? No! Of course not! Why?"

Brad shrugged, embarrassed to have revealed something, even if he wasn't a hundred percent sure what, and relieved that Duane really seemed not to be mad at him, but also freshly worried; maybe there was something *really* wrong. "Anything that I can...? I mean, I know it's not like I can probably *help* with anything, but, you know...."

"No, it's nothing like that. But I do need to...."

Duane trailed off; a hubbub was advancing towards them: another splinter group from the Instagram Tour. Guys. Five of them, guys in their early twenties with neon-dyed buzz-cuts and T-shirts emblazoned with the logos of obscure, hip "start-ups" that in reality were no doubt funded by mega-corp money. The way they flung the doors open and strode in, three abreast, still shouting their conversation, reminded Brad of a cocky football team striding into a locker room. Not that Brad had ever been in a locker room, unless the v-brothel antechamber counted. On second thought, Brad didn't think these guys had, either. They just knew from watching shows and commercials and vids how such jocks were supposed to behave, the same way Brad did. If they hadn't learned the behavior from the same clichéd sources as Brad, if they really had picked up their manners and mannerisms from immersion in some social cabal from which Brad had been excluded, then he wouldn't have recognized it all so clearly.

Neither Brad nor Duane were strangers to noise, but the thunderous guffaws and shouted comments jarred so much with their mood of a moment earlier that they both jumped. "Look at the faggy rainbow shit!" shouted one guy, delighted, waving at the watercolors.

Squinting, another one shouted, "Dude, these are pictures of boats!" Brad had the urge to point out to the guys that, actually, lots of the watercolors did not depict boats. He held his tongue, horrified that such a bizarre intervention had occurred to him at all.

The revelation that the pictures were of boats provoked cheers of joy from the sharp-eyed faux-jock's four companions. They started shouting jokes about homosexuals and their prevalence aboard boats. As if they'd rehearsed it, three of the guys hopped in front of a watercolor of a sunset at Cannes and posed for a picture, all of them in profile: the guy in the middle pretending to get butt-fucked by his buddy standing behind him, and the third guy on his knees before the butt-fuckee, pretending to blow him. The two flanking guys, butt-fucker and blower, flipped off the camera. The guy in the middle turned toward the lens, eyes bugging and crossed, jaw distended, tongue sticking out, as if the whirling violent sensations had driven him totally nuts. It all happened so fast that by the time the photo got snapped, Duane and Brad were only just leaving. The guy standing with beefy arms crossed beside the photographer stage-whispered to his buds (or maybe he really did believe he was legitimately whispering), "Check it out, we ran off those two faggots."

Back in the Cypriot hall, the couple from earlier had gone. But the wannabe-jocks' hooting and screaming was so loud that there might as well not have been a door between them. Generally, neither Brad nor Duane gave a second thought to ignoring that kind of noise, particularly in public, but those dudes seemed like people to avoid. So they wound through the halls till they got to the Chinese lacquer room. They stood before that big red platter with all the details and the pictures of kids, that Brad had stared at for so long the first time he'd come here with Duane.

Finally Duane said, "Um, but. So, what I was going to say...."

In the flush of escaping the invasion of their Signac room, Brad had forgotten about all that. "Oh, yeah, of course. I'm sorry...."

"No, don't be sorry. *I'm* sorry. It's about," and here Duane took a big swallow of air, as if prepping to get through what he had to say in just one breath, "it's about the Pence Academy—we've been given new limits on how many students we can recommend—and I'm worried that it might affect Katie."

"Oh," said Brad. Knowing the answer, but hoping this might be one of those times where he was wrong, he asked, "Affect her, how?"

"Well, originally, they were going to let us recommend fifty kids from our Consolidated. But now they've cut the number to fifteen."

"Oh. How come?"

"They gave the other thirty-five slots to the Consolidated Four district."

Brad nodded reasonably, even as rage sent headache-inducing amounts of blood crashing into his brain. Consolidated Four contained Meerville's highest tax brackets. So in a way it was natural that they should get the lion's share of slots—but by the same token, why the hell were they screwing around with such a rinky-dink place as the Pence Academy? Folks like him aspired to the Pence Academy—Consolidated Four's people ought to be aiming for much higher spheres, and leaving the Academy for Brad's little girl and boy!

"Well," said Brad. "That sucks."

Duane nodded solemnly. "Yeah," he said, and returned his gaze to the lacquer platter.

The relief in Duane's voice alarmed Brad. He seemed to think the subject was closed. And that the whole thing had gone more smoothly than he'd feared. Hurriedly Brad said, "But, so, are you worried it'll be harder to get Katie in, now that there are less slots?"

Duane blushed. In a carefully casual tone, he said, "Yeah. I'm afraid so."

"Okay. Well. I know you'll do your best. It's cool."

Duane crossed his arms over his chest, took a step back from the display case, oriented his body to face Brad's. "I would love to help Katie get in. I really would."

"I know. Don't worry, nobody expects, like, miracles. I know you'll try."

"The thing is, there's not a lot I *can* try."

Brad felt his face grow hot again. He forced himself to stop blinking. "Can't you just sort of bump her up a little higher on the list?"

"Not really, I'm afraid. Not with her academic record. When I had fifty slots, I could fudge her test results enough that they made up for the grades, at least enough to get her in among the bottom. But for me to justify getting her into the top fifteen...." Duane shrugged.

Brad made himself unhear that Katie's test scores had needed to be "fudged," even to get her into the bottom rungs of the top fifty. "Okay, well," he said, then stopped. He couldn't think of anything to say, but simply giving up was unacceptable. "Well." No obvious tactic announced itself. Except, he suddenly realized, trust. "I know you'll do the best you can."

The dismay on Duane's face told Brad he'd been right: if there was any way for Duane to help him, the best way to spur him on to it was to simply continue counting on him. Part of Brad regretted injecting bad feeling into this burgeoning friendship—but only in the dim, irrelevant way a starving man might fret over the conditions at the poultry factory where his chicken sandwich originated.

His understanding of how badly Duane wanted to help only made it more nauseating to see how he squirmed; if he wanted so badly to make things right but still wasn't going to do anything, then the situation must really be fucked. Duane said, "I'm sorry, I really am. But I just don't think you should count on anything from my end."

Brad nodded. Now his face was a different kind of hot. He wondered what it would be like if he started crying in front of Duane. As a grown-up he'd never cried in front of anyone before, and he didn't know the protocol.

He cleared his throat. "Okay. That's cool. Only, I may bring it up again later, if that's okay. Just if I think of anything to suggest that we maybe could do. Just, it would make me feel better to know you wouldn't mind that."

Duane nodded and said "Sure," though he looked worried.

"I don't want to hassle you. I know you don't owe me anything. It was wrong of me to ask you, even."

"No, not at all. Why do you say that? I was glad you asked. I mean, I would love to help you, if I could."

"No, I know."

A lull. Brad had the sad sense of not knowing why they were here in the museum. The whole idea had been to get Katie into the Pence Academy, right? Now that that was kaput, why bother?

Then he felt guilty. What right did he have to decide it was kaput? What kind of father did that make him? This was his daughter they were talking about.

"Just, if I could reserve the right to bring it up later," he repeated, keeping his tone utterly harmless.

"Of course. But like I said, I'm not sure there's going to be anything that I can do."

"No, I know. But just, like. If we could agree that some possibility might turn up. In principle, is all."

"In principle, sure," said Duane, with a shrug. One could agree to anything, in principle.

Nine

Brad prided himself on his professionalism. Took it for granted, even. So he was well into his next fuck-session with Duane before he even realized there was a problem. And once he did, there wasn't enough time left in the session to get back on track.

Not that there was anything anyone could point to, anything Duane could complain about. Not only did Brad blow and then fuck the guidance counselor expertly, he was even warm with him. Seemingly warm, anyway. He said the right things, asked the right questions, smiled with the correct degree of gentle affection.

But the sexbot was a subtle tool, amply well designed for conveying an actual human presence remotely. Brad's job was not merely to run through a checklist of actions and remarks, but to feel the truth of them. Sometimes a degree of fakery was necessary, and Brad could do that expertly. But over the weeks Duane and the sexbot persona called Becky had cultivated a real intimacy, meaning Duane could tell something was off.

Brad was so good at going through the motions that he himself might not have realized how little of his heart was in it, had he not seen the lack reflected in Duane's distress. Duane grew steadily more worried and solicitous, until Brad had trouble making him come. He debated faking an orgasm himself; normally there would be no question but that that was the thing to do. With Duane, though, and Duane's niceness, he gambled that acknowledging his own inability to reach orgasm would, perhaps perversely, help repair the damage his spiritual absence was doing to their intimacy.

"What's wrong?" asked Duane, mournfully.

"Oh, nothing—nothing with you, anyway." Hearing the transparently false note in his voice, Brad realized that, actually, he *wouldn't* mind Duane knowing it was his fault. It was Duane's refusal to go further out on a limb for Katie that kept Brad's head out of the game. Wishing Duane to feel responsible was clearly insane, since it wasn't as if Brad could give him any hint of *how* he was responsible—Duane learning that Brad was the one driving the sexbot would fuck things up on multiple levels. Yet he couldn't shake the irrational impulse.

Duane blinked. He looked down at his wet, twitching penis, just emptied. Brad knew he was feeling guilty for having let himself indulge in such pleasure when his partner hadn't managed to share it.

Brad's heart softened, like sad wax, and he started to move toward Duane, with his arms and his spirit. But then he stopped himself.

He had no plan. Only the sense that an unsatisfied soul was more likely to spur itself back into motion. Brad didn't know what good Duane could do him; even if Duane tried to please the sexbot operator, he was unlikely to do so by making a special effort to get Katie into the Pence Academy, because he had no idea Brad was the operator. On the other hand, nothing could be gained by Duane's complacency. And with his children's future at stake, Brad couldn't neglect even the most pathetically slim possibility.

So he held himself in reserve. Smiled at Duane, was friendly. But held back something neither man could define, though both could feel.

Duane said, "Nothing with me—but so something *is* wrong?"

"I'm really sorry, I shouldn't even have let on that anything was up. That by itself is already a breach of contract." There was no reason to say that, except to twist the knife a bit, by reminding Duane of the professional nature of their relationship, of the absurdity of whatever emotional content he'd invested it with. It surprised Brad to hear himself; it seemed a bit of useless cruelty since, again, it wasn't likely to occur to Duane that the way to get back in the good graces of his sexbot operator was to sneak Brad's kid into the Pence Academy. And if there was no utilitarian purpose, then it didn't make sense to hurt Duane—because Duane was his friend, right? And yet Brad found that he didn't mind hurting him. He'd had the chance to salvage the future of a child, Brad's child. Sure, at some risk to himself, but weren't certain things worth a risk? For example, a child? Especially the child of a friend.

"I don't care about that," said Duane. "About breach of contract, and all."

Brad almost laughed, almost pointed out that it was all very well for Duane not to care about it, but Brad was the one who stood to lose a job; their entire relationship was subject to contracts; the one Brad had signed with the v-brothel, and the one Duane had agreed to when he'd pushed "Accept" after the Terms and Conditions, back when he'd signed up for his first visit. Luckily, Brad stopped himself. Saying all that might have been enough to drive Duane away from the brothel for good.

Brad just shrugged (prettily; he made it a pretty shrug without thinking about it, out of habit). "It's just personal stuff," he insisted, apologetically. "No kidding, I really shouldn't let it interfere."

Duane began a movement toward Brad which he immediately restrained. "But I … I mean, I don't want to overstep, or be a creep. I know that our relationship has parameters, and I, you know, respect that. But *I* don't mind that personal stuff. If you wanted to broach it. I mean, I don't mind if you don't, either."

"Oh, thank you, Duane. That's really sweet." They were entering dangerous territory. He and the clients had both been assured that no recordings were made of the data being shuttled back and forth between Brad's suit and the sexbot, and that no humans were listening in. No way to know that for sure, though. Besides, an AI *was* listening in—for the safe word, but who knew for what else? No telling when some conversational pattern might trigger disciplinary protocols, might persuade the AI that Brad had strayed from approved comportment guidelines and broken his contract. If that happened, he might be fired right away, without any human review, even.

"It's sweet," he repeated. "But this time is meant to be for you."

Duane recoiled into himself like a burnt slug. What the fuck was he doing, Brad demanded of himself? If he drove home to Duane that he was exploiting Brad, that theirs was a money-based relationship that existed solely because Brad had been hired, then he really would drive Duane off. Duane wouldn't harbor any resentment, wouldn't judge Brad—it would be himself he would judge, guilt which would drive him off. Guilt, and the shame of having indulged in so foolish an illusion.

Brad's income would take a hit. More than that, though, he realized he would miss Duane. Even if his everyday persona continued to hang out with Duane, go to the Arts Center and baseball games and so forth, he would still miss their fuck-sessions.

But those sessions were tainted now. Brad had let himself grow lax. He'd failed to adequately compartmentalize. And now, if he hoped to repair their relationship here in the v-brothel, he wondered if he might have to go to the source of the rift, out in the everyday world.

Ten

Just before the fuck-session ended, in its final few minutes, Duane said, "I don't mean to make you uncomfortable. By trying to get you to break the rules, or anything like that. I mean, *I* understand the need for discretion. If people at *my* job found out I was going to, you know, a place like this, then I'd be in a lot of trouble."

Brad only nodded understandingly. He'd scared himself by almost making a reply that would have revealed he knew Duane's job; that was how leaky the barriers between personae had become. As the session ended and Duane melted from Brad's eyes, he could feel Duane picking up on his freaked-out energy, and getting even more worried and frustrated.

Back in his "real" body, Brad trembled as he peeled off the suit. Hopefully the weirdness of his interaction with Duane had raised no flags with the monitoring AI.

He had a couple hours free before he had to pick up the kids. Once home, he wondered how he should spend the time. The question made him anxious. Soon he'd eaten up so much time trying to figure out the answer that it was time to go get the kids, anyway. The car wouldn't start so he had to spring for a cab—on the way to the school he kept slapping the ads off every time they resumed, but once he had Katie and Keith in the car he didn't bother. They were so rambunctious that it wasn't as if there was any hope of peace and quiet. And anyway, now that the kids were with him he wanted the noise, to crowd out the thoughts of what was likely to happen to them without Duane's help.

At home, Brad wanted them all to watch a video together, as a family. But neither Katie nor Keith would deign to even consider the other's choice, and when Brad couldn't stand their shouting any longer he gave in and allowed each child to watch his or her own program on his or her own tablet. All three of them sat on the sofa, Brad slumped on one end, Katie in the middle and Keith beside her, each kid absorbed in a blaring tablet; Katie was watching a dubbed Korean cartoon, Keith a montage of airplane crashes. For a long time Brad's eyes dwelled on Katie, and he let his mind wander; then he pulled out his own tablet and began scrolling through headlines from the entertainment newsfeed. Wow, he hadn't had time to see *any* of these movies or programs.

An inbox-alert blooped onto his screen. He tapped the icon, and blinked; it was from Duane.

Before even scanning the message, he felt fear. Weird, to get a message from Duane, so soon after their fuck-session. It amped up his earlier, worrisome sense that his system of compartmentalization was breaking down.

The message said, "hey, u want 2 hang out?"

Brad's heart warmed. Then he looked at his daughter and that affection curdled. Here they were, he and Duane had this rare and cool thing, and Duane was fucking it up by not doing all he could for Brad's daughter. Brad knew he was being unfair; still, he couldn't shake off that way of feeling things.

He wrote back, "im with kids 2nite, sorry."

He hit Send. Then, once the message was gone, an idea struck him. True, he couldn't go out and leave the kids, but.... He examined his inspiration from as many angles as he could; then tapped out, "but u cd come hear, after they r n bed."

He sent that message, too, then tried to go back to perusing the Entertainment headlines. But the Inbox screen pulled him back, then kept him fixed there. Never mind that if and when Duane replied, he would get an instant notification. He couldn't help but stare at the tablet, waiting. When had been the last time he'd invited someone who wasn't even family over to his home, for no good reason? Probably not since he was a kid, and of an age appropriate to mess around with stuff like friendship.

Maybe Duane would be shocked or freaked out and wouldn't write back. Well, fine; Brad wouldn't even blame him. But he wouldn't let himself feel embarrassed, either. Duane was the one who'd asked to see *him*. Brad felt morally justified in responding to the invitation as he had, even if socially it was unusual.

But then Duane responded: "ok. wt time kids go 2 bed? i come after."

Breathless, Brad's eyes darted over the shabby, disordered apartment: a guest! Coming *here*! In the first exotic flush of the thought, he felt the urge to tidy everything up; but the mess was too sprawling and deep, plus cleaning would freak out the kids. Which would make it even harder to get them in bed before Duane's arrival. Anyway, if he and Duane were really going to be friends, then Brad shouldn't try to disguise who he was and how he lived—at least, he had a vague sense that's how it ought to be. And, while it might bruise Brad's pride for Duane to think he lived in a dump, in a way it gratified his vanity for him to know that Brad hadn't taken any special trouble for his visit.

He texted Duane back that the kids' bedtime was ten—actually, they generally stayed up as late as they wanted, and ten was when *Brad* tended to conk out. The text sent, and it being only eight, he started bracing himself for the epic struggle of getting them into bed by nine-fifteen (he was sure he would need the cushion). At eight-thirty he told the kids they would have an early lights-out; they flipped, and for over an hour the apartment hosted a storm of tears and screams. By nine-forty, Brad had managed to grind them down. Once they'd been wrestled into their pajamas and bedroom, he gave them each a soporific and watched carefully to make sure they swallowed them. That done, he turned off the light and closed the door to their bedroom, fairly confident they wouldn't be bothering him again—one of those soporifics could knock even him out within ten minutes, and he was way bigger than either child.

He settled in to wait.

From his lonely vantage on the sofa he regarded the mess anew. Wrestled down the urge to hop up and try to make a dent in it, after all. No point, too late.

Duane might not even show up, anyway.

But he did, right on time.

At least, he was right on time as far as Brad was concerned. But as he entered, the first words out of his mouth were to apologize for being late. Brad noticed that, indeed, it was four minutes past ten.

Not that it relaxed him, exactly, but Brad was grateful to see that Duane was as flustered as him. It made things less lonely. Why was meeting at one of their apartments so different from meeting at the Arts Center? More intimate, he supposed. A non-public space, not meant for anything but living in, a space with no presentational function.

"Uh." Brad tried to conjure some sort of protocol guidelines from memories of old vids. "Can I get you something to drink?"

Duane clearly wasn't certain how he was supposed to respond. "Like, what, for example?"

"Um. Water. Or there's juice. The kids' juice."

"Juice, I guess."

"Okay." Brad took the three steps to the fridge in the kitchen nook, opened it, and grabbed two cans of the kids' apple soda. (They'd be pissed when they awoke and found them missing—Katie and Keith kept scrupulous track of their sodas.) But as he handed a can to Duane he saw an apologetic frown on his face. "Oh, sorry," said Duane, "has that got caffeine in it?"

Brad looked at the can. "Uh. Probably." He wondered if Duane had thought he'd meant *real* juice, and not fruit soda.

Duane pretzeled his mouth. "I actually try not to take caffeine after dark," he said, as if explaining some mildly offensive religious tenet. "It stops me from getting to sleep."

"Oh." Brad knew, in a theoretical way, that caffeine kept you up, but it had never occurred to him to try to apply that knowledge to real life. Maybe he, too, would sleep better, if he quit drinking it at night. "Sure, okay, but, uh…. Gee, I guess the only other thing we have is water."

"Sure, water's fine."

"From the sink, though," It was Brad's turn to be apologetic.

Duane couldn't prevent a slight, disgusted pursing of his lips. "Maybe just nothing, then. Sorry."

"No, no. I'm the one who's sorry."

After a bit more of that sort of thing, they wound up on the couch. Brad couldn't help but be paranoid that they were going to wake up the kids. Probably Duane was yet more paranoid about it; visiting students' parents at home, after dark, might not exactly be against the rules, but it was unusual enough to draw attention if found out, for example by Katie and Keith spotting him and spreading the word. And getting attention drawn to yourself was never a good way to hold onto a job. But the kids were not going to wake up, not with that soporific in their bloodstreams. Meanwhile, the fact that Duane would run such a risk merely to see him gave Brad a warm feeling, one that coexisted uneasily with his resentment over the refusal to slide Katie into the Pence Academy.

Of course, the most obvious reason for Duane to have come over would be to explain that he was going to try to do just that, after all. That possibility had sparked a glowing excitement within Brad. But it clashed with Duane's apologetic, guilty air.

Why had he come, then?

They plowed through some small talk, each of them laboring to keep the conversation plodding along, like an ox-led cart through a muddy field. (That was an image Brad had once seen in a clip from some old movie, and for some reason it had stuck with him.) It occurred to Brad that if he quit making an effort at small talk, it might force Duane to come out with whatever he had on his mind. He stopped advancing topics, even the weak ones he'd been trotting out so far. When Duane asked him lame questions about his day or put forth cute anecdotes, Brad replied with monosyllables, or grunts. He held fast against the temptation to smooth things along. At last Duane realized he was going to have to actually come out and say the hard thing he'd come to say.

"Look," Duane began, then gulped down a large breath. "Listen. I just wanted to come over and say how sorry I am about the Pence Academy thing."

A flutter of hope in Brad's chest; Duane had come about the Academy, after all. He waited for the next part.

Duane leaned forward, making a nebulous gesture with his hands. "*Really* sorry."

Oh. There was no next part. He'd just come to say sorry, because he felt guilty. But what really struck Brad was the continuity between his gestures earlier, at the end of their fuck-session, and the yearning his whole body incarnated now. Naturally, you would expect a lot of continuity: it was the same guy, on the same day. But it was the same guy talking to a different person. Generally, people adopt different personae depending on who they're with. This had been the case with Duane up till now; there had been a difference between the Duane who interacted with the sexbot and the one who, say, had met Brad that one time in the guidance counselor's office. Now it was as if that difference had collapsed.

Duane was sitting there, waiting for a reply. Brad opened his mouth but got no further. What would he say? His reflex was to wave dismissively, to say "That's cool." But he couldn't do that. It wasn't cool. Regardless of whether or not Duane's decision not to push for Katie's entry was ethical, *Brad's* duty remained clear: he was supposed to get his kid into a higher sphere, by any means necessary.

Duane kept waiting, gazing at him with hope and distress. Fear, even. Brad peered more closely at him. Déjà vu: this genuinely was the same expression Duane had directed at the sexbot earlier, when he'd wanted Becky to be less upset.

Something obvious and impossible occurred to Brad.

Maybe the reason Duane was wearing the same persona with everyday Brad as with sexbot Brad was that he knew they were one and the same.

A crazy idea. But why else should he show up here, so frightened of Brad's displeasure? As frightened as he had been of the sexbot's? With the sexbot it had made sense—any ordinary guy would be upset at the idea of screwing up such expert fuck-sessions. But what possible thing could he be so scared to lose, that he got from just plain Brad?

Then there was the timing. They'd just had that awkward fuck-session a few hours ago. It had ended with Duane trying to draw out the Brad of the sexbot. Now here he was, talking to everyday Brad as if picking up where he'd left off. Coincidence? Seriously?

The notion that Duane might have found him out sent a complicated thrill through Brad. Fear comprised part of it—willingly or not, if he'd revealed his identity somehow then he'd committed a serious breach of contract, one that could immediately void his franchise license.

Then again, it didn't seem like Duane was holding the leaked secret over his head. In fact, he seemed to be going out of his way not to come out and mention it. (Brad had to remind himself that this might be because Duane had no idea Brad and the sexbot were one and the same.) Almost as if he wanted Brad to know that he knew, without making the knowledge official, so that they could continue on as if they did *not* know.

A long shot. How in the world would Duane have figured any of this out? Then again.... Brad himself was highly sensitive to the slightest shades of behavior. When he was operating the sexbot, at least, if not in his everyday persona. Perhaps Duane shared that gift. Perhaps he'd noticed some infinitesimal tic, some tiny mannerism, shared by the sexbot and Brad. Brad's professional pride rejected the idea, but his rational mind had to admit the possibility.

If Duane had figured out that his "friend" Brad was also his favorite sexbot operator, then this errand made sense. He'd sensed that the attack on Katie's future had screwed up Brad's equilibrium, and he'd come to patch up their relationship so that his blow jobs might once again be not merely perfect, but warm.

Okay. Brad could understand that.

He understood that the question was complex. No one appreciated the power of compartmentalization better than Brad; he understood that (assuming he was correct at all) it was open to speculation how conscious Duane was of his knowledge. As a heterosexual male of a vanilla profile, he was unlikely to openly confront the intuition that his valued sexbot's operator was a male. Maybe on some level he had figured it out, and had accepted the need to act; but he would want to keep that level below the surface.

Despite Duane's evident desire to make things right between them, he seemed to have no clue how to do it. He just sat there on the sofa, repeating himself: "I just wish I could express to you how sorry I am."

Brad laughed, ruefully, and with an unkind bite. "Well, I think I have a pretty good idea. Because I'm equally sorry. More, even. I mean, it's my kid."

Duane blushed. "No, of course. I'm sorry."

Brad hesitated. Showing a little anger was all right, he figured. It would help negotiations if Duane understood that Brad was angry. Also, if he and Duane really were "friends," maybe it was okay to be open about how they felt, anyway, to a certain extent. But he couldn't *just* be pissed off. Duane did have a real problem: how to get Katie into the Pence Academy, without getting himself fired. Maybe Brad could sort of be his partner in solving this problem. Like, Duane wouldn't have to feel that he was all alone in working it out. It would be a team effort, not just a demand Brad was placing upon him.

Adapting a more reasonable tone, he said, "Well, anyway. I understand they've made it way more of a challenge."

"They've made it impossible." Duane said it with fear, and with desperate courage, like a man leaping from a burning high-rise and hoping to land in the swimming pool below.

"Impossible?" It wasn't so much that Brad didn't believe him, as that it was his duty not to believe him. That added a little sneer to his voice, for the first time in their acquaintance.

Duane responded with wounded defiance: "I could lose my job."

"But you wouldn't *definitely* lose your job."

"No, I wouldn't *definitely* lose my job, I would just *probably* lose my job!"

Suddenly Brad heard their conversation as if he'd been an outsider. Who the hell did he think he was? "I'm sorry," he said, meekly ducking his head.

Duane softened. "No, don't be. Like I said, I'm the one who's sorry."

"I know there's no.... I mean, I know I have no claim on you where I could ask you to risk your job."

Duane's face twitched in a sort of despair, like there was a point of vacuum within its center, tugging at his features and distorting them. Brad understood that Duane wanted it to be possible for someone to have such a claim upon him, that he would have liked to be in the sort of relationship that produced such a claim, but that reason and all his experience of social life assured him it was impossible.

Duane said, "There are still opportunities here at the public-school level, though. Programs Katie could be taking advantage of, that I could get her into."

"Okay."

Duane told him about these programs, at length, padding out with excess vocabulary their lean spots. Brad listened, nodded, saying "Cool" and "Wow." Despite Duane's sales pitches, the programs sounded like wastes of time. It was clear to each guy that the other thought so. They weren't trying to fool each other with their enthusiastic words, or fool themselves. They were just sticking to their scripts, because for the moment they had nothing else.

Eleven

A couple days later they met again at Zack's. Brad sprang for a taxi, so that this time he could get drunk. He informed Duane by text that he was going to do so, trying in a non-pushy way to hint that Duane should join him in a bit of intoxication.

What about the kids, though? Between the cab fare and the prospective bar tab, he couldn't spring for a sitter without running the risk of coming up short on rent. Ellen wasn't available. Brad did some agonizing, trying to parse out to what exact degree he was being a selfish dickweed and negligent father. But he truly was acting on behalf of the kids. Say there really was a risk in leaving them alone, without a sitter. In the long run, wasn't the risk of being stranded in the anonymous masses worse? Getting them into the Pence Academy might spare them that. Things were bad enough now, and there was no telling how shitty they might get in the next fifty or sixty years. According to the long view, he was doing the most responsible thing.

Not that Katie saw it that way. "You're not supposed to leave us alone here," she scolded him, bitterly. "It's illegal."

"It's not illegal." In fact it was illegal. "But it is private, though. So don't mention to anyone that I did it. Okay?"

Katie crossed her arms over her chest. She angled her body away from him and glared straight ahead ferociously. "It's not safe." Keith hung back, hiding in his tablet, busy being inconspicuous on the sofa. Brad could feel him willing his big sister to shut up and let them just enjoy their few hours of unmolested freedom. "What if a criminal or a killer comes by?"

"Then you'll leave the door locked." Brad hastened to add, "Anyway, a criminal or a killer is *not* going to come by. Why would they?"

"To kill us."

"That's not going to happen. Listen…." He trailed off. He wanted to explain that he was doing this for them, that he had to set things up so that he could get drunk, in order to create an emotional situation where he could make his pitch to Duane. But how could he explain something like that to a nine-year-old and a seven-year-old? "You just have to have, you know, faith. That I'm doing this for you guys. Even if I can't explain how or why, exactly."

Disdain oozed down Katie's face like slime.

Brad splurged and got a drink before Duane even got to Zack's. A shot, not a beer—he figured that would get him tipsy faster, and for less money—he drank it fast so that he could get rid of the shot glass, so that Duane wouldn't realize he was setting out to get *drunk* drunk. Not at first. By the time Duane did show up, Brad had a regular pint glass of beer before him.

"Hey," said Brad, grinning big, patting the barstool beside him. Duane sat, with a timid half-smile. Brad interpreted the smile as hopeful that this get-together was Brad's way of indicating the bad time between them was over, and simultaneously worried that instead it was Brad's next salvo. Brad was so touched by how deeply Duane felt this thing between them, he forgot to feel guilty over the fact that it was indeed another salvo.

"Hey," said Duane, timidly, asking forgiveness.

Brad indicated his pint glass. "Did you see my text?"

From Duane's squirmy look, Brad could tell he knew Brad was referring to his intention to get drunk. "Yeah," he said. "Fine with me."

Self-conscious, afraid Duane would ask what business it was of his, Brad said, "So … how about you? Are you down for…. I mean, I don't guess you also took a cab?"

Duane looked apologetic. "I drove here, actually. I wasn't sure I could really afford the fare. But you go ahead, and don't worry!" With his hand he waved away any scruples that might be lingering in the air around Brad's head.

Brad tried to loosen his face enough to smile. Fine, he *would* go ahead—it sucked to go alone, was all. A prickling in his brain told him he was already on his way. It had been a long time since he'd drunk a shot. He pulled the pint closer to him and drained half of it in one draw.

Duane signaled the bartender to bring him a pint, as well. While the bartender's attention was on them, Brad also gestured for another.

Now Duane was watching him a bit warily. He said something, but it was lost in the blaring techno and general hubbub. Brad shouted at him to repeat himself.

"I said, What's up!" cried Duane, leaning in close to Brad to deliver the message.

Brad shrugged extravagantly.

Duane flicked another nervous glance at the almost-empty pint glass. "You felt like spending some money tonight?"

Brad shrugged again, nodded, shrugged. Their drinks showed up. Duane handed the bartender a thirty-dollar bill, paying as he went instead of opening a tab as Brad had done. Brad was startled to find that his own pint glass was already empty, and ready to be swept away. He took a swig of the new one, then said, "You know what I usually do? With my money? Instead of drink it?"

"No, what?"

"I don't know if I should tell you, actually. It's kind of, you know...."

"You can tell me. I mean, unless you don't want to."

"It's weird. Or, no—it isn't, actually. A lot of people do it. But it's embarrassing."

"What is it?" asked Duane, after waiting to make sure Brad wanted him to ask.

Brad took another long draw on his pint. Jeez, this new one was already more than half gone! "Well, I actually ... man, I can't believe I'm telling you this.... I actually spend a lot of time going to v-brothels."

Duane didn't say anything.

"You know?" said Brad. "With the sexbots?"

"Yes, I know what they are," said Duane. Looking around, he added, "You might not want to ... well ... be so loud."

"Why? Do you think there's anything wrong with it?"

"No no no no no no no, it isn't that. Only, uh, I mean you yourself just said you were afraid of it getting around."

"These people are all strangers, I don't care what they think. I said I was worried what *you* might think of me, because we're friends." Only the alcohol he'd already consumed allowed him to come out and use the word "friends" like that.

Duane blushed. "Yeah. Thank you. I mean, yeah, we are, I think."

"But so you.... I mean, what do *you* think about it?"

Duane shook his head, opened his eyes wide, rotated on his stool to face his beer, and generally made a show of not being the one to ask. "I'm not the one to ask," he said. "But I think, you know, there's nothing *wrong* with it. I mean, it's—uh—it's all consensual. Just, people can be weirdly judgmental, is all. Like, even if I did want to do that—I mean, not that I have anything against it—but even if I did want to visit a v-brothel, I don't think I would. Because of what could happen if people at my job found out."

Brad held his eyes on Duane. "You wouldn't visit one?"

"Well, no. Not that there's anything wrong with it! In fact I can understand how it could be really, you know, uh, not even mainly about the sex." At the word "sex" Duane lowered his voice so much that Brad couldn't actually hear it, although he could tell what it was thanks to context and the movement of Duane's lips.

"Oh? What do you think it would be about, instead?"

"Well. Emotion." Duane seemed even more embarrassed by this word than he had been by "sex." "But I mean, I don't *know* that, I'm just imagining...."

"No, no, it's cool. I'm just interested that you would say that. Because most people, you know, it's not what they would say. What, uh, what made you think of that?"

"Well. I mean. Gosh, I don't know. It's a lot of money, right? It would be weird if people paid that much just for *pleasure*. I mean, the whole point is that there's a person on the other end."

"Oh, you don't use the cheap option and just have an AI run the sexbot? You pay all that extra for the remote human operator?"

Duane looked at him with the still regard of a child whose adored father has just shown the first signs of a tantrum. "I told you. I don't go to v-brothels."

"Oh, sorry, that's right." He signaled the bartender for another beer. "I guess these drinks are going to my head."

"Uh. Maybe you should slow down."

"What? I told you, I'm celebrating. You knew I was going to be drinking a lot, I told you."

"Yes, that's true. What are we celebrating?"

"A break in my long stretch of never celebrating anything." The bartender replaced his empty pint glass with a full one. Brad got to work on it. In his peripheral vision he saw how Duane's gaze followed the glass from the counter to his mouth, carefully, the way a guy scared of flying stares out the window at the wing of a plane, willing it not to fall off. Not that Brad had ever been able to afford an airplane ticket anywhere, that was just a cliché he'd picked up.

Duane said, in a neutral voice, "Well. I guess that sounds like a good thing to celebrate."

Brad didn't reply. Just nursed the beer. Duane waited.

Finally, Brad said, "But, yeah, so anyway. You're right. I do always spring for the remote human operator. Because, I mean, I know it's silly. An AI could do pretty much all the same stuff. Only, I like feeling like there's a connection."

Duane waited until he was certain he was supposed to respond. Then he said, "Sure."

"And in fact—I mean, you're really going to laugh at me—but in fact I pretty much always book this one particular operator."

"Sure." Duane plainly wished they were talking about something else.

"Maybe," Brad added with a snort, "it's just that I'm too broke to shop around for anything better."

For a moment it seemed like Duane wasn't going to respond. But then, in a tone very different from Brad's, as if he were somewhere else having a separate conversation, he said, "You probably feel a real connection to this person, whoever she is."

"You really think that's possible?"

"Of course. Why not?"

"But it makes me a sucker. Doesn't it? To take seriously a relationship like that? With someone who doesn't even know who I am? That's based totally on money?"

"If it feels to you like there's something real between you, then that's probably the case. You can't fake things like that."

Brad gave the sort of cynical laugh he hadn't uttered since the last time he'd gotten drunk. "Oh, you don't think that can be faked?"

"No," said Duane, getting a little prickly. He hedged his bet: "Not usually, anyway."

"I can fake that kind of stuff."

"I don't believe that." Now Duane sounded really angry. "You don't seem like the kind of person who could do that, even if you tried."

"Anyone can. Just, some people are better at it."

"No."

Brad knew why Duane was so outraged at the suggestion that Brad was a skillful bullshitter; the idea that their friendship might be bullshit stung him. Had he been sober, Brad might have been moved. As it was, he felt only a bitter curl of resentment: their relationship was important enough for Duane to get mad over a simple statement of reality, but not important enough for him to slip Katie into the Pence Academy.

Of course, Brad knew Duane couldn't just do that. Sounded like even if he stuck his neck out and got himself fired over it, Katie still wouldn't get in. But Brad had no right to think that way, regardless of what he did or did not know. His duty was to fight, and in order to fight he had to believe he might win.

His beer was already empty. He signaled for a refill. Fuck it. "She and I show each other sides of ourselves that we can't really show in normal social situations," he said, apparently forgetting that he'd just implied all that was bullshit. "Or he, maybe. It's not like I know for sure what gender the operator is."

"You would know," Duane said. He didn't sound certain, though. "You would be able to tell."

"Would I?" He started in on the new beer, uncertain how many this made. "What I wonder is, would I recognize that operator, if I saw him out in the world? Or her? It feels like I ought to be able to tell just by looking into the person's eyes who it is. Because of how intimate we've been. It feels like, if I happened to find myself talking with that person, even if they were in a totally different body, even if they weren't physically similar to the sexbot at all, I would still be able to tell it was them. Just because of something in the eyes. Just because of the mannerisms. Or I don't know—something like that, anyway."

Brad stopped talking. He drank down half his new pint. He looked over at Duane, a little frightened.

Duane just sat there. Not looking at him anymore. Beer unfinished. He seemed to wake up, reached out to caress the cold wet glass with trembling fingertips. Said something in a raspy voice Brad couldn't hear. When Brad asked him to repeat himself, he said, "I think I better go." His voice stayed raspy, but to make the words audible Duane put so much force behind them that they almost sounded violent.

All Brad's bravado had been made of alcohol fumes, and Duane's words swept it away. "Oh, really?" he said, pathetically. "I thought we would hang out."

"I don't think I'm going to be able to keep up with you. Like I said, I drove here, I didn't take a cab. And even if I had, I don't think I would be able to keep up."

"You should finish the one you ordered, at least."

Duane, already risen from his barstool, stared at the pint glass. Clearly he didn't want it. But in ordering it he had made himself responsible for it, and he would feel guilty leaving it undrunk.

He blushed, and anger soured his features. "You can finish it," he said, politely. "It'll save you a little money."

He'd already moved a pace away from the stool. "Okay," he said, firmly, self-conscious over that firmness. "I'm going to take off."

"Well." It wasn't pride that kept Brad from asking Duane not to leave. He just couldn't figure out how to ask it. But he sensed this was a catastrophe. "Okay." A sick-feeling headache was shrugging its way up to the surface. "See you soon?"

"Yeah, sure," said Duane, backing away.

"Like, just the usual? The Arts Center, or something?"

By now Duane was too far away to hear him over the music and all the ambient noise. Still, he nodded and said, "Sure"— Brad could tell by reading his lips that was what he said. Duane turned and left the bar, walking quickly, not looking back.

Twelve

Brad woke up, sick with alcohol, sicker still with the knowledge of what he'd done. He swallowed both sicknesses down, let them burble in his gut, roiling up bile.

He went about his business. Dropped the kids off at school. He was so sick that he once again took a self-driving AI cab. Katie hardly spoke to him—she was digging in on this whole thing about how he shouldn't have left them alone, and he could tell she would keep milking it. On the way from the school to the v-brothel, he sat in the back of the cab, head tilted back, eyes closed, hands atop his thighs, trying to keep a handle on his nausea, holding it with a loose grip, afraid a tight one would knock loose something wet and smelly inside him. He banished from his mind all thoughts of how this cab fare was driving him into yet more dire financial straits, after last night's fares and unheard-of bar tab. He banished lots of things from his mind.

Today he had a full schedule. It had been booked solid for a week. Four sessions, about all he could handle before it was time to go pick up the kids again; he liked at least a quarter-hour to decompress and recalibrate between each session. Some variety, today: he was the male dominant in a homosexual BDSM thing; the male in a heterosexual "sweet-romance-style" fuck-session; a female in a stridently egalitarian lesbian coupling; and the female in a highly patriarchal, rape-tinged hetero one-on-one. Despite his hangover, he comported himself quite well throughout all the sessions. He could feel that he was a bit off, but none of the clients were able to tell a difference. Duane would have sensed something, but not these strangers.

Speaking of Duane, he was scheduled for a session tomorrow, during his mid-day break. All day Brad held off on checking his account, until he was through with his last session. Then he looked and found exactly what he'd been dreading: Duane had canceled the next day's appointment. Brad's hangover finally proved too much for him, and he rushed into the v-brothel's tiny toilet and vomited.

In the cab back to pick the kids up from school, he agonized over whether to send Duane a text. He couldn't let it appear that he was texting in direct response to Duane's cancellation; he needed some wiggle room for deniability, for them to be able to feasibly pretend that Brad had not revealed what he had revealed. He decided to go ahead and send the text. It was amply believable that he would be texting merely to apologize for his behavior of the night before, in his everyday persona.

So he sent a text saying, "hey sory 4 last nite if i got 2 drunk." Then, seconds later, one which read, "lol."

He waited. For a long time Duane didn't reply. Not really such an abnormally long time. Except Brad knew Duane's schedule pretty well, and he ought not to be busy right now.

Maybe he just wasn't going to reply to any of Brad's texts anymore?

At last, though, he did. Brad's inbox blooped. By now he was with his kids, and he tried not to let them perceive with what desperate eagerness he opened the text; but both kids were absorbed in their own tablets, Katie in a video game and Keith in a car-chase vid. Duane's text said, "no prob."

Not the warmest message. Still, maybe everything was cool. Maybe the cancellation was only a coincidence. Sure, Duane was probably annoyed at him for being an obnoxious drunk, but maybe that's all it was.

Brad figured he ought to leave it alone a while. For nearly ten minutes he managed to do just that. Then he couldn't help sending another text: "around next wk or 2? maybe go 2 arts cent.?"

Again the wait was long. At the end of it all he got was a text saying, "kinda busy."

He thought he might throw up again. He managed to keep his face stone-still; his kids wouldn't have noticed anything, even if they'd been paying attention.

Now, for real, he ought to just leave it. For twelve and a half minutes he left it. Then he sent another text: "o wel, thats cool. see u @ basball game."

He waited, waited, waited. No response. Whatever, though; he'd see Duane then. Brad had already bought the tickets, for both of them, and that meant Duane would have to go.

Anguish corroded through him at the idea that he might not see Duane until the game. That was almost two weeks away. But that was all right. They were just going through a bad patch.

After that, he timidly refrained from texting his friend. Each moment of each day was stretched out with the suspense of waiting for Duane to send him a message, and the despair of knowing he wouldn't. A week passed. At least the game was coming up. Except that the text Duane finally did send was disastrous: "hey brad looks like i cant make game. if u cant find som1 else 2 use my tick i can pay u back 4 it."

The deal had always been that Duane would pay him back, that they were going dutch, that Brad was putting both tickets on his card just for convenience's sake. The idea of going by himself was too sad to fully visualize. The idea of inviting someone else was such a joke, it almost made him actually laugh. Who? Ellen? Brad knew that Duane knew how absurd the suggestion was. Given Duane's nice-guy hangups, that he had gone ahead and made it anyway told Brad, for the first time, just how committed he must be to breaking off their friendship.

Staring at the screen of his tablet, Brad forced his breathing back under control. This was bad. But not necessarily a disaster. Duane did want to break it off—this text was proof. But Brad could get him back. Because Duane was a good guy. Good guys can be manipulated. But it would only be manipulation at the very first, only until they were actually physically together.

Duane was trying to avoid seeing him—okay. But the reason he wanted to avoid seeing him was so he could hold on to his anger. The whole point being that he figured, if they did see each other, he wouldn't be able to hold on to it. Well, Brad would just take him at his word. He'd just have to set it up so that they did see each other, was all. No need to panic.

It called for groveling. Brad didn't especially like to grovel, but he didn't mind because he knew that Duane wouldn't be able to resist it. Still, as he started tapping out the text, he felt a regretful resistance dragging at his fingers. He didn't like to let this note enter his relationship with Duane. Normally, if circumstances called upon him to beg, he could defend himself by harboring a little nugget of secret contempt within himself for whoever he was begging to. But he didn't want to have contempt for Duane. He couldn't quite muster any. And that left him defenseless against the humiliation of prostrating himself.

He wrote: "plz? pretty pls? lol. just dont think i can findd replacmint is all."

He waited. Four minutes went by with no answer. Totally reasonable, not a long lag at all. Felt eternal, though. Suspecting he'd be better off not doing so, he couldn't help but add, "wd b cool 2 see u again, anyway. lol."

Duane responded, at last: "ok."

A little bubble of joy floated up, clearing a path for itself through the misery-snot that had accumulated in Brad's chest; "rilly?" he texted back, tacking on a smiley face.

A few minutes later Duane replied again: "i said, ok."

Thirteen

Only a week remained until the baseball game, so Brad decided to be cool and not bug Duane till then. Not overly bug him, anyway; he forwarded him a few memes. He figured that as long as he wasn't adding any comments, it wouldn't be annoying the way normal communication would be. Brad wanted to keep up *some* form of interaction, so that once he and Duane made up they could more easily pretend this gap had never happened.

Meanwhile, of course, Becky also passed the week without seeing Duane.

At long last, on Saturday, Brad texted to say, "c u 2morrow @ game. outside gate 4." Sending the text felt like an exile's first tentative steps home.

He didn't hear back. Had Duane missed the text and forgotten the game? Refusing to let himself text yet again for confirmation, he walked around with his fists clenched, not realizing he was doing so till Katie pointed it out.

Next day, Ellen showed up as promised to babysit the kids. Soon he was waiting outside Gate Four, trying to look nonchalant, keeping his sweaty palms shoved into his pockets, the crowd of baseball fans milling past him into the stadium. Just a small stadium; Meerville wasn't host to any big-league games.

And there he was! Duane! Brad grinned—then, when Duane didn't grin back, refrained from pulling his hand from his pocket to wave.

Duane had his hands in his pockets, too. His face was blank. Brad kept his grin pasted on. He would have liked to walk towards Duane, put an end to this suspense, but he didn't want to be too forward.

At last they were face-to-face. Duane just stood there, looking at Brad with that blank face. Finally he said, "Hey."

"Hey!" said Brad. He pulled his tablet out of his pocket and waved it. "I got the tickets. You wanna go on in?"

Duane gave a just barely perceptible nod, as if to say that, yeah, that was why he was here, after all.

Brad nodded too, pumping his head up and down, as if it were an enthusiasm-generating machine that he was trying to prime. He pointed to Gate Four. "Well, you wanna go for it?!"

Again Duane gave the almost invisible nod. "Sure."

Brad led the way, resisting the urge to twist his head around every few steps to make sure Duane was still there. *Act normal,* he kept telling himself, *act like nothing's wrong.* Be cheerful, but not *too* cheerful.

Be cool. He couldn't understand why he was having so much trouble properly calibrating himself. At work, in the v-brothel, the key to his high ratings average was his expertise at generating an appropriate state of mind. Why couldn't he carry that skill over into his mundane persona?

He flashed his tablet screen over the reader at the turnstile. The turnstile let him in, but then refused to understand that the second ticket in his account was meant for Duane, and locked him out. Brad started tapping buttons on the cracked, dirty screen of the turnstile, trying to explain to the AI what was up. Gate Four had only two turnstiles, and though the baseball game wasn't exactly mobbed, a bottleneck started to form. Most of the thwarted ticket-holders waited with dull, unmenacing apathy—ticket-checking AIs fucked up all the time, after all. Yet Brad could feel the pressure emanating from the crowd as his fingers fumbled across the keypad, pleading with the AI. Worse, he could feel the pressure from Duane. He stood there, hands in his pockets, waiting dumbly, but with his lips beginning to purse in an impatient way that was not characteristic of him. Brad felt sure that Duane was on the verge of saying something like, *You know what, let's forget it, the AI's not gonna let me in,* and turning to walk off. At last, the

AI allowed Duane through the turnstile. The drama had taken almost two minutes.

They went up the ramp, walked to their narrow seats. Now that they were situated, Brad let the novelty sink in of being in a chair outdoors, of settling in to regard an outdoors spectacle. Although the game was scheduled to begin soon, the stadium was only sprinkled with seated attendees. Guys played catch in the field. Brad knew that wasn't part of the game proper. This was called "warming up."

He grinned at Duane, finally giving himself permission to look directly at him, now that they were sitting next to each other. "I don't know who the Meteors are playing today," he said. "Not that I would probably know, anyway. I don't really keep up with the sport."

Duane kept his gaze on the field, not as if he were particularly interested in it, but simply as if that were a place to put his eyes. He shrugged, as if to say that *he* certainly didn't know who the Meteors were playing, nor could he care less.

Brad nodded, not to signify agreement with anything, simply continuing to pump his head. "But so," he said. "What have you been up to?"

Duane shrugged again. Still wouldn't look at him. But he remained too polite to simply not answer: "What do you mean?"

"I mean, the past couple weeks. What's been going on?"

"Nothing. Just the normal stuff."

"Well. I just thought, maybe you'd been busy. Since normally we would have hung out some."

This time, Duane didn't reply.

Brad's face got hot and a headache bloomed. "I mean, not that we *have* to hang out. I mean, I just…. Um. Anyway. Have you, like, been to the Arts Center?"

"You know why we haven't hung out."

The bottom fell out of Brad's belly. But it couldn't be as bad as it sounded. No way would Duane actually come out with all that stuff. Calling his bluff, because he suddenly felt sick of this powerless, pathetic feeling, he said, "Well, no, I don't know, but it's cool. I mean, it's not like we can't be busy sometimes, and it's not like … I mean, it's not like we *have* to hang out—there's no reason to … I mean, not that there's no *reason*, obviously there's a *reason*, but there's no, like, *obligation*, is all…."

While Brad was getting tongue-tied trying to articulate the nebulous unwritten expectations of the shadowy social state, "friendship," Duane's jaw was getting tighter. In the middle of Brad's stumbling babble, he interrupted: "It's because of what you said about the v-brothel."

Brad's whole body was simultaneously flash-frozen and burned to a crisp. He went rubbery inside. The only hope lay in continuing to pretend not to know what Duane was talking about: "What, you mean about how I, how I go to the sexbots? Listen, man, I didn't mean to offend you, I just get lonely sometimes is all. Plus I was drunk…."

Finally Duane turned to look directly at him. His eyes were red—shit, he looked like he might be about to start crying! *"You're Becky,"* he said.

Brad gaped, horrified and awed that Duane had actually come out and said it.

Then only horrified. Because how could it now be unsaid?

Duane scowled at him, waiting for him to say something. Brad just let his mouth continue to hang open. His original plan had been to depend on Duane to be motivated to help Katie by his subliminal awareness that Brad and Becky were the same—but he'd counted on that awareness *remaining* subliminal. Unspoken. Not that he'd really thought about the "plan," such as it was, since that night at Zack's.

Duane's scowling mouth pulled in on itself tighter as he realized Brad wasn't going to reply. He turned back to the baseball field.

Music had started. Big, goofy organ music with only a little bit of static. Players were running out onto the field.

Brad assumed Duane just wasn't going to talk to him anymore. So it took him aback when he said, still glaring at the field, "How come you wanted to meet today, anyway?"

"Well. We've been talking a while about coming to this game."

Duane spat out a sigh, that told Brad he'd been expecting something more. Or felt he deserved something more, anyway.

Brad said, "Or, we could, I mean…. I mean, did you want to talk about this other thing?"

Duane kept glaring at the field.

"Look, I just, uh, I didn't *plan* it. You just got assigned me, was all. And then, when I wanted to hang out with you, it wasn't for anything, uh…. I'm not a pervert, is what I'm saying. I just wanted to help my kids. At first, I mean."

Duane didn't reply. An even stronger bitterness stained the bunched muscles of his mouth. Whatever he wanted Brad to say, Brad wasn't saying it.

"It's not like I ever really *lied* to you," said Brad.

Duane's head whipped back toward Brad. "Are you kidding me?! Is that a joke?!"

Brad glanced around nervously, but nobody seemed to be paying attention to them. Nobody sat in the chairs right next to them. The soundtrack of organ music blared, and the scattered spectators cheered on cue. "There's things I didn't come out and *tell* you, but I didn't ever *lie*."

"That first time. What I asked. You remember?"

Oh. He meant when he'd asked Becky if she were really a girl, on the sexbot's other end, and Brad had given his usual canned answer. Brad blushed and looked down. It was on the tip of his tongue to insist that he *still* hadn't lied, not technically— the canned answer was calibrated so as to not technically be a lie. But he felt like that level of hair-splitting might infuriate Duane even more.

Besides, that wasn't the defense he would have used. It wasn't that he hadn't technically lied. It was that he felt Duane had been in cahoots with him for the lie, sort of. Surely, deep down, Duane had known the canned reply was bullshit, that there was a strong chance a male had been operating the sexbot. He must have seen enough vids about the industry to have a vague idea how it worked. He must have been savvy enough to know that his question and Brad's response were just a bit of role-play to help make the fantasy function. Brad felt that Duane had been in on the joke, and it seemed uncool of him to now insist he hadn't been.

Duane sat waiting for something. For an apology, Brad supposed. But Brad balked at offering one—he'd only been doing his job. Once he realized Brad wasn't going to give him anything, Duane stood up. "Excuse me," he said, "I have to go."

Brad fumbled himself upright to follow him. "Wait! At least watch the game."

"I looked it up—baseball games can last *hours*. I reimbursed you for my ticket—I'll reimburse you for yours, too."

"Why should you pay for mine? That doesn't make any sense." In saying so, Brad was aware of being generous. Since Duane was the one spoiling this outing, he *should* have to pay for it. He should have to pay. The affection Brad had dared to let himself cultivate these past weeks, finding itself thwarted, easily curdled to animosity. Dismayed, Brad watched it curdle, unable to prevent it. If Duane insisted on fucking everything up instead of going with the flow, then maybe he should have to pay.

Brad tamped down those personal emotions. Following Duane, he plucked at his shirt and said, "Listen, if you want to go, that's fine, but I'd like to please talk about Katie and the Pence Academy first...."

Duane spun around. He looked like he really might punch Brad. "There *is* no Katie and the Pence Academy!" he hissed.

They'd stopped in front of a group of four guys, one row further up. "Down in front, faggots!" said one of them. Brad and Duane shuffled fifteen feet further along the narrow aisle till they arrived back at the concrete ramp they'd entered by. Now that they had more space and weren't blocking anyone, Duane once again turned to Brad.

"There *is* no Katie and the Pence Academy," he repeated. "I told you this before. I tried to tell you nicely. With her grades, aptitudes, and IQ, there is no possible way I can justify making her one of the fifteen students I recommend. Even adding her to a list of the top fifty could have gotten me in trouble. But it's a risk I was willing to take, because we were friends."

"I don't think that's a very fair thing to say about Katie. I don't believe there's any way she's not in the top fifty of that school." Never mind that the question of whether she was in the top fifty was moot, now that she had to be in the top fifteen. "She's gifted."

Duane rolled his eyes. "Brad, Katie is *not* gifted."

"How the fuck would you know? I live with her, she's my own kid. Have you ever even met her?"

"I don't need to meet her, I have access to all her scores and meta-data."

"Well maybe if you knew how to do your job you'd be able to read those scores the right way."

"If *you* knew how to do your job we wouldn't be having this conversation! How would you like it if I told the v-brothel company about you, huh?"

"About me what?!"

"About you following a client around out in the real world and trying to use our time there to blackmail me into helping your kid, that's what!"

Brad almost threw up, partly from the pain of having their relationship summed up that way, partly from terror at the thought of what would happen if Duane really were to make such a complaint. "That's not fair," he moaned. "How can you call it blackmail? I never even told you that Becky and I were the same person."

"Then how the heck do I know it?!"

Who knew how long they might have stood there spitting accusations and lame excuses at each other. What got them unstuck was the realization that a chubby fifty-something man had moved down to the end of his row, just beside the ramp, and from ten feet away was holding up his tablet and videoing them. As Brad and Duane stared at him, wondering how much of their fight he'd recorded, the guy made no acknowledgement of their noticing him; he continued to concentrate on his screen, keeping them properly framed. No doubt their public tizzy was unusual enough to warrant being recorded and then uploaded onto this guy's YouTube and RollSnap accounts. Without another word Brad and Duane hastily descended the ramp as the guy videoed their exit, panning along to follow them.

Once outside the stadium, Duane said "Stop following me!," loud enough to embarrass Brad.

"I'm not following you, I'm just leaving at the same time."

"Well, don't." Brad realized Duane was crying when he took his glasses off so he could scoop the tears from his eyes with his fingers. "Just leave me alone," he said, and scurried off.

Fourteen

He tried to kill time before going home; he didn't want the humiliation of Ellen and the kids knowing he'd left the game early, that for some reason his mysterious outing had been cut short. He found a free parking space in a neighborhood far from his own. He got out of the car, walked about thirty yards away, and sat on the sidewalk. He leaned against the wall, midway between two derelict ATMs. If he sat in his car, someone who wanted the space might start honking at him to try to get him to move. Pedestrians bustled past him. Most people noticed him in time; a few, their eyes fixed on their tablet screens, tripped over him. Brad felt barely more than dead. He didn't even take his tablet out of his pocket.

After two hours, he got up and returned to the car. Might as well go and relieve Ellen.

Back at the apartment, the kids and Ellen all had their tablets out, playing different vids. At first Brad couldn't figure out why Ellen didn't get up and leave as soon as he walked in. Slowly he realized she wanted to socialize. He clamped his jaw down on his exasperation; if that was how she wanted to be compensated for the trouble of watching the kids, well, okay.

The kids barely looked up from their blaring tablets as the adults sat in the room with them, mostly wordlessly. Ellen wore gray sweatclothes with pink piping. Her graying blonde hair was cut short and stuck out every which way. She looked like she'd aged ten years since Megan had died, and for the first time Brad noticed how weird she seemed to be getting. They sat there a long while, not quite making eye contact, trying and often failing to resist the urge to pull out their tablets and look at them. At last Ellen stood up abruptly. Muttering something that sounded like "Bye," she left the apartment with the jerky, shuffling gait she had developed.

After she left, Brad picked a fight with Katie, first insisting that she show him all her homework for the weekend that she'd completed, and then, since naturally she had not completed any of it and didn't know what the assignments were, announcing that her personal tablet time would be strictly rationed. She wouldn't be allowed to use it for anything until after she'd completed her homework. The idea of taking someone's tablet away was unheard-of; it took a while for Katie to even understand the threat, and once she did she began shrieking. Brad lunged to snatch the tablet. She pivoted, keeping it from his grasp, baring her teeth.

Brad paused. This could escalate; Katie really would bite him. Anyway, he didn't need to physically confiscate the tablet. He had full access to her account settings, theoretically, since he paid the internet bill and the account was in his name. If he fiddled a while with the settings, he ought to be able to figure out how to limit her usage, and force her to do her homework.

He sat on the sofa, taking his own tablet out and hunting through the icons for the account settings. Keith also was on the sofa, scrunched into a ball on its other end, eyes glued to his own tablet screen as he scrupulously avoided noticing their fight. Katie watched Brad warily, till she satisfied herself that he'd given up trying to steal her tablet. She eased herself into the armchair and started playing a video game. Its bloops and dings filled the room, since Keith's tablet was on mute. The better to avoid being noticed.

Brad gave his son a hard look. If Keith saw it in his peripheral vision, he was careful to give no sign. Brad couldn't tell what kind of video he was watching, could only see the colored lights spilling across his face.

"Everything I said to Katie goes for you, too," he warned.

Keith gave no sign he had heard. Tried his best to give no sign he even breathed.

Brad finally managed to get to his account settings. The dashboard was a complicated snarl, and navigating it was not made easier by the advertising windows that kept popping up and having to be closed. Blocking all ads, of course, would require paying for the premium service, which Brad could not afford.

The struggle to change the account settings occupied all his spare mental power. The capability had to exist for a parent to control his child's internet access. But the option wasn't offered in any straightforward way—wasn't stated outright in any drop-down menus or anything like that. Naturally they wouldn't make it easy, even if they legally had to make it possible; it wasn't in the interest of any powerful entity to have ordinary people spend less time on the internet. Brad kept opening tabs that either led nowhere, or else back to the snarled dashboard page. Calling the customer-service hotline would entail at least a one-hour wait, according to the menu. That was annoying, since he'd be talking to an AI and not a human, and since AIs could handle multiple transactions at once it seemed like an AI should be able to pick up right away.

Another ad popped up, distracting him from his hunt for a path through the account settings, prompting him to look up again at Katie, where she hunched sullenly over her bleeping, blooping tablet. "That doesn't sound much to me like you're doing homework," he said darkly.

Katie didn't reply.

"Jeez, what a waste." He loaded his voice with as much sarcasm and contempt as he could, to shame her into changing her ways. "I mean, you have no idea, do you? You have all this potential. You have the chance to actually be a person someday. But do you think that chance is going to just hang around waiting, if you don't get off your butt and do something to grab it? Huh-uh. No way."

Bleep, bloop. Katie kept her scowl on the screen.

"You're gonna find out the hard way," he said. "Ninety-nine point nine nine nine percent of the people in the world are crap. Just crap. Do you know how hard it is to be one of the point zero zero zero zero one percent who actually get to do stuff they want to do? Even if you *have* potential, it's the hardest thing in the world to become one of those people. And here you are, you have the chance to actually be one of those people someday. And why are you throwing it away? Because you're too lazy to do your dumb-ass fucking easy homework. Well, one day, when you're eating out of garbage cans, and hiring yourself out as a test subject for experimental drug treatments because there's no other jobs you can get, you'll think back on this, about how I was right, and you'll wish you had done your homework. I'll be dead by then. I know you'll probably be glad I'm gone, but you'll still wish you'd listened to me and done your homework. Except you *are* going to do it, because I'm going to fucking make you."

What do you say to something like that? Katie must not have known, because she said nothing.

Brad didn't know what else to say, either. He just sat there, sad and confused that not even such a speech had been able to reach his daughter. He didn't know what else to try. Except maybe hitting her; and he had a sudden vertiginous view down a long tumbling tunnel of violence. He shook it off, spooked. Went back to trying to decipher the dashboard stuff. Finally he gave up and scrolled through his RollSnap account a while, before heaving himself up off the couch and into his bedroom, without saying good night to the kids.

Fifteen

Next morning he didn't bother saying anything about the new tablet rules as he drove Katie and Keith to school and dropped them off. Wouldn't be any point, till he could deliver on the threat. None of them exchanged a word, from the time they got out of bed to the moment he dropped them off at school. He continued on alone to the mall.

Maneuvering through traffic, he yearned to be able to afford a self-driving car; he would be able to sleep through his commute, or at least veg out; these commutes made up the bulk of his alone-time, and it didn't seem fair that they should be eaten up with driving. Plus he'd save money in the long run, because with a self-driving car his insurance costs would plummet. If only he could get over that initial hump of the first down payment. Just get six months ahead or so. But who was he kidding? He couldn't even manage to keep this piece of shit running well enough to not need a cab every other month.

At a stop light he grabbed the chance to shut his eyes and massage them with his thumb and forefinger. Well, maybe if he put in yet more hours at the v-brothel. Would be a strain, both mental and physical, but he could handle it. Would also mean more time away from the kids, and if he sprang for a babysitter that would basically eat up whatever extra money he managed to bring in. Well, once in a while he would just have to leave them alone in the apartment. They were old enough, more or less, and he could lock up the apartment from the outside—he'd just have to decide which possibility scared him more, that of the children being trapped during a fire, or that of the children being able to leave the apartment and wander where they liked (or being vulnerable to one of those roaming killers Katie insisted on believing in, who were always checking apartment doors to see if they were unlocked). And he could always call Ellen. She seemed to need the fiction that she had some meaningful relationship with her niece and nephew. With her brother-in-law, even. Maybe he would even bring her in on the secret, let her know he was a sexbot operator. She would be grossed out. But her practical side would understand that Brad could make a shitload more money at brotheling than he could at anything else, and she would, perhaps grudgingly, respect his ability to provide. And the act of taking her into his confidence would be a salve to her loneliness. Yeah, she could be brought on-board. Become almost a partner in the family. Sort of a surrogate mother to the kids, one Brad wouldn't need to have sex with or spend much emotional currency on. Once he got in the habit of the extra work, and she got in the habit of helping with the kids, who knew what opportunities might pop up. Brad couldn't see how he would ever manage to earn enough money to actually make a real difference to anything— it wasn't as if brotheling would ever bring in enough to, say, pay the tuition at a higher-echelon school. But maybe a little extra money could do something. Money could always do *something*.

Brad knew he was spinning out these industrious fantasies to distract himself from the door that had slammed so tragically between him and Duane. Well, so what. He had to find some new way forward. He still had years and years to trudge through, probably.

He parked at the mall, right next to the entrance. The parking lot had always been nearly deserted, but today, as far as he could tell, the lot was *completely* deserted. There had to be a few employees' cars, stashed somewhere—maybe over on the other side of the building? In any case, the mall's days definitely seemed numbered. What would happen to the v-brothel when the mall was finally shuttered? If they had to transport the facility somewhere else, would they take those expenses out of free-lancers like Brad's cuts?

Entering the mall, bass-heavy music thudded into him, smothering the mall's official soundtrack. Mounting the dead escalator, Brad got to the second floor and saw that same group of hoodlums from a few weeks ago, from the day he'd first fucked Duane. Anyway, he thought they were the same. They noticed him, and eyed him with hostile curiosity. Or maybe it wasn't hostile, maybe that was just Brad's imagination. Maybe they weren't even hoodlums. Why did Brad think they were hoodlums? Because they were black, was all, and because they played their music loud. But why shouldn't they play it loud? There was nobody here in the mall to be bothered by it.

As he walked by them, he nodded, curtly, business-like. He figured that would be better than keeping his eyes straight ahead, like he didn't even see them. Now there was no mistaking the mockery with which they regarded him. But that still didn't make them hoodlums. They could tell he was scared of them, for no good reason. Why shouldn't they mock him a little for that?

In the clothing store there was a new employee, a chubby Asian teenage girl behind the counter. She watched him walk in with open shock at seeing a customer. Yeah, this clothing store was not long for the world.

No time to fret over it now, though. He needed to be fucking in twenty-two minutes, as an extremely dominant heterosexual man. Had to get himself into the proper headspace.

He went to the back, as if headed for the dressing rooms. Went to the brothel antechamber instead. He ran his card through the reader.

Nothing happened. Absolutely nothing—no red light, no refusing beep. That made Brad think the machine was dead. Shit, in that case how would he get inside in time for his appointment?!

He yanked his tablet out of his pocket. On the verge of swiping past his incoming-messages window to access the Call screen in order to call Hardware Support, a message caught his eye: from Kaufmann-Berlini. Probably nothing to do with this broken door, but he opened it anyway.

A restraining order.

He was warned to not come within one thousand feet of his former place of employment. This place, the v-brothel. Forever.

"No," he whispered, as his trembling fingers tried to call up his dashboard. "No no no no no no."

He was locked out of the dashboard. He couldn't even get to a frozen copy so that he could at least see it, see his upcoming appointments, see his ratings average.

Hands really shaking, he placed a call to the troubleshooting hotline. At least the AI picked up right away. Brad replied orally to its maddeningly long string of prompts; several times the AI blandly informed him that it hadn't understood and an answer needed to be repeated, probably because Brad felt naked and exposed, out here locked out from the v-brothel and its antechamber, so he kept whispering his answers, and the pounding music in the background made him inaudible.

While talking to the AI, he swiped back to the messages window and took a second look at the e-mail from Kaufmann-Berlini. Mostly gobbledy-gook, but severe gobbledy-gook. One sentence read: "The former contractor is further reminded of his/her NDA, and that any further violations thereof may lead to prosecution, even if legal action is not pursued for past violations."

What past violations? Brad's skin puckered with sudden cold.

The AI said, "Your account has been permanently frozen and you have been barred from any future professional dealings with Kaufmann-Berlini." Brad nearly shat his pants. Not from fear, but like a dead body whose bowels open at the moment of death. They hadn't even bothered to program the AI to say all this with an ingratiating tone and a hypocritical apology.

"Why?" demanded Brad, no longer whispering. His voice came out rough and hoarse.

"Your account has been permanently frozen and you have been barred from any future professional dealings with Kaufmann-Berlini."

"Yeah, but *why*? And what about my customers? I have people I'm supposed to see *today!*" It wasn't even about himself and his problems, he wanted to explain—what the AI ought to keep in mind was the needs of his poor clients.

Now that the prompts had led the AI into this cul-de-sac, it wasn't going to leave it: "Your account has been permanently frozen and you have been barred from any future professional dealings with Kaufmann-Berlini."

Brad hung up and stood there, hunched over the tablet, squeezing it in his fists. Clenching his jaw so tight it felt like he would break his teeth. What would happen to his clients today? They would show up and he wouldn't even be there. And his ratings would take such a hit that once he did get all this sorted out he'd have to crawl his way back up.

Except the company must already have a plan for that. They would have gone ahead and let him service these four clients and then fired him afterwards, if the alternative had been to lose them. No doubt some other operator had been assigned them. Everyone *thought* they could tell the difference between one operator and another—that was the whole point of rating individuals. But that was bullshit. Ninety percent of people wouldn't tell the difference.

Possibly Duane would have been able to tell if someone other than Brad had tried to be "Becky." But even then.

Hell, they could probably just have an AI do the fucking and the talking, and no one would care.

Only now did Brad start to really ask himself what had happened. He'd had so many nightmare visions of losing his job that it felt at first like the fulfillment of a prophecy, with no particular need for an explanation—just another random floating tragic injustice. Now he began to ask himself how this could have occurred.

A lot of stress had been placed on NDA's in those messages he'd been sent.

No doubt that was part of Kaufmann-Berlini's boilerplate language.

But.

Did they think he'd violated the NDA? By telling someone he ran a sexbot? Had someone sent them an e-mail telling them so?

Fist clenched, Brad reared back, raising the fist to the low ceiling and giving out a cry. Except it wasn't really a cry: more of a strangled, muted thing, high-pitched, that would have been nearly inaudible even without the booming music. He remembered Duane's threat to go to the brothel and accuse him of having followed around a client out in the ordinary world.

He did it! He did it! Brad's face was sticky and wet. *He really fucking did it!*

He tried to convince himself that something else had happened. But the threat had been too explicit, and the timing couldn't be coincidental. Befriending Duane had been the only unprofessional thing Brad had ever done. The only other contender he could think of was that time he hadn't gone ahead and let that guy beat the shit out of him, and that hadn't even been technically against the rules.

The savagery of it left him out of breath. One thing, not to help Katie. Another, to make Brad lose his job. To fucking starve him and his family and put them out on the street!

Brad wanted to ask him why. He also wanted to kill him.

He tried to call up the keypad screen on his tablet—his hands were shaking too hard. Whole body was shaking. Like a seizure. Brad didn't really give a shit if he had a seizure, except that he wanted to call Duane. He braced his body against the wall, pushing his whole left side against it with all the strength of his legs. Pressing his left arm against the wall as hard as he could, the arm that held the tablet, he managed to get its shaking kinda-sorta under control. Then with all the concentration he could muster he was, eventually, able to call up Duane's contact info and press the Call button.

All that, to not even get a ring tone. Only a prim computer saying, "This subscriber has blocked all calls and texts from this number."

Motherfucker! Cocksucking faggot bitch!

A drop of something splashed onto the screen of his tabet—he didn't know what it was and didn't bother wondering (it was his own sweat). He didn't even know his teeth were bared. He called up the contact info for the kids' school. Only the main switchboard's number was available, and following all the polite automated prompts to the guidance counselor's office nearly drove him insane. At last a human female picked up: "Can I help you?" You could tell it was a human from how bored and annoyed it sounded. Probably that same secretary who had scowled at Brad that one time.

"Yes, I need to speak to Duane Wilkes."

"What? I can't understand you."

Fury was twisting up his mouth muscles and distorting his voice. He forced himself to smooth them out. "Duane Wilkes."

"Who?"

"The guidance counselor."

"Oh. Wait." An uncanny void on the line as she put him on hold. She came back. "He's not here," she said. While Brad was asking when he'd be back she hung up.

He cried out again. This time the fat girl at the store's front counter would have heard him if the music hadn't been blaring. He slammed his forehead into the wall, twice. Staggered back out of the little corridor, groping his way along through the bursting stars and colored blobs obscuring his vision.

Before the hoodlums had even noticed him he was screeching at them: "What the fuck are you looking at?!" They burst out laughing. He kept screeching as he stalked by at double-time: "What the fuck are you looking at, faggots?! Faggot bitches!" Once he called them faggots they stopped laughing and got serious. But they didn't do anything. Maybe he looked really crazy.

He peeled out of his parking space. The car's computer started beeping at him; he forced himself to slow down and follow the traffic laws. If he got into a wreck right after the car had warned him about his driving, then his insurance would refuse to pay anything. Not that anything so rational penetrated the crimson puke-fog he was groping through. If he *had* been able to articulate anything clearly, he would have said that he couldn't afford to get pulled over or have a wreck until after he had fucked that motherfucker Duane right back, just the way he himself had been fucked.

If he marched in there and started yelling to everyone in the office about how Duane had come down to the v-brothel and eaten Brad out and let his dick get sucked, how long did anyone think they'd let the guy stick around? It would be justice. It would have been justice even if Duane *hadn't* gotten Brad fired, because Duane really was a shitty guidance counselor—just look at how he'd let down Katie. Whereas Brad had been amazing at his job.

Even if he couldn't breach the school's defenses, even if he had to stand out front and yell at passersby about how he'd fucked the guidance counselor, that would be enough to get Duane fired. The school couldn't have people yelling shit like that. But just getting Duane fired would not be enough. Brad wanted to be face-to-face with him when it happened. Look him in the eye.

See him again.

Suddenly he was at the school, with no real memory of the drive.

As he came out of whatever trance he'd been in, it was like he left all his energy behind him, all his will. He stared at the school, gripping the steering wheel to keep himself upright. Pictured the confrontation with Duane, felt the reality of it swell within him with orgasmic nausea. He'd march to the office. He'd already be making a scene, though no one yet would have guessed the bomb he was about to drop. Duane, hearing his voice, would rush out of his office to head him off. His eyes would be full of fear, but also pain. He'd walk up to Brad and stammer—no, he wouldn't stammer—he'd say, in a voice grown rich and mellow with suffering and regret, *I shouldn't have done what I did; I acted out of pain.* And then Brad would tear up, as he was doing right this very moment here in the car, and he would say.…

Brad shook the vision off, suddenly afraid; he felt himself slipping into a belief in this dream of reconciliation. Soon he'd be believing he could get his job back. Trying to work back up the rage that had been sustaining him, he started to open the car door, then his eyes flicked around nervously—what if Katie happened to be nearby, and spotted him? He slumped back onto the seat.

He looked at the school. He wasn't going in there.

He and Duane were never going to see each other again. Because even if he did go in there, even if he did make a big crazy scene, big and crazy enough to physically draw Duane out of his office, Duane wouldn't really *be* there. He'd pretend not to know Brad, or to only barely know him—he certainly wouldn't admit to being his friend.

Not even getting Duane fired would bring him back. He wouldn't seek Brad out, look him in the eye, say, *I didn't realize the pain I was causing you until it also happened to me, and I'm sorry.* He'd just be out there somewhere, fired, and for Brad it would be like he didn't exist.

Brad punched in the code to restart the ignition. As he backed out of the parking space, he tried a new fantasy, a heroic fantasy, where he set noble eyes upon the section of the building containing Duane's office, and wished his former comrade luck. He couldn't manage that, either. But he did manage not to feel anything, at least.

Sixteen

No one ever bumped into each other in Meerville. That was why it felt like such an event when Brad and Duane did.

Brad exited the drug-testing facility out onto the strip-mall parking lot just as Duane was about to enter. They both came to a halt and stared at each other dumbly.

Brad nodded over his shoulder. "You going there, too?"

"Yeah."

In order to be eligible for the government-assistance lottery, you had to not only have an income below a certain level, but also pass randomly-scheduled drug tests; a text message would pop up on your tablet, warning you that you had a two-day window in which to submit to a pee test or you'd be kicked off the list. If that happened, you'd have to recommence filling out the miles of application forms from scratch.

Brad wasn't sure what to do with this moment, but he felt that simply ignoring it would be cowardly and a waste. "You want to, I don't know, talk?"

"Sure," said Duane, quicker than Brad had expected.

Again, Brad nodded towards the testing facility. "You want me to wait while you?..."

"No, no," said Duane. "I'll come back later."

Brad got the impression that Duane was afraid he'd find Brad gone, if he tried to make him wait till after the pee test. That anxiety gratified him. Plus he was relieved, because you always had to wait at least forty minutes for your chance to pee in the cup. Theoretically, the facility's total automation precluded the possibility of human error and its attendant delays. But the "clients" provided plenty of human error, there being a fairly high contingent of broken-down wrecks who could eat up long stretches by arguing fruitlessly with the aloof computers, or by missing the receptacle when they pissed and then, instead of stepping aside to yield their place to the next person, standing there dully until their kidneys spat out a fresh batch of urine. Even without such salt of the earth getting thrown into the gears, the place was just plain overbooked.

Still, Brad heard himself politely saying, "You sure? I'd hate to mess up your schedule...."

"No, no, really. I have till tomorrow. And I have nothing else to do."

Looking at Duane more closely, Brad noticed that his jacket and hat looked pretty shabby. This was January, and it had been well over a year since they'd last seen each other at the baseball game.

Brad looked around. Across the four-lane street was a Starbucks. Eyeing Duane worriedly, he said, "You want a coffee?" He couldn't afford to buy Duane's coffee for him.

Indeed, Duane's face got tight with something akin to fear as he looked at the Starbucks. Clearly, he couldn't really afford to buy his own. But he must have really wanted to talk to Brad, because he said, "Sure."

Cars and trucks zoomed by on the four-lane road separating them from Starbucks, but the nearest traffic light was nearly a quarter-mile away, so they dashed across. The gaps in traffic were small, and the guys did not calculate well; they might have been crushed by an oncoming truck, but luckily it was self-driven, meaning it slowed down upon perceiving two humans in front of it.

The Starbucks turned out to be full of bums, and people who wanted to get in out of the cold without buying anything. The AIs that ran the Starbucks weren't equipped to do anything to actually force people out; simply, a grating alarm was sounding constantly, and over it a loud nasal voice kept repeating, "This Starbucks is for the use of paying customers only, please—all others please exit." Over and over, it repeated this. Folks generally ignored it. Except for one twenty-something woman with curly blonde hair and wild eyes, holding a latté she'd actually paid for, and yelling, "I spent money to have someplace quiet to sit and drink my coffee, and there aren't even any seats and you people are setting off the goddam alarm! None of you should even be here, I'm the only one who's paid for anything! *None* of you should be here!" She must have already seen the place was crowded when she first entered; dimly, Brad wondered about her thought process.

Brad was quite happy not to have to buy anything. Duane actually sighed, murmured "Thank God," and let the muscles of his shoulders visibly relax. Some Starbucks outlets sprang for an actual human security guard, to enforce the customers-only policy. But the corporate cost-benefit analyses must have decided to sacrifice this one.

No seats were available, as the blonde woman with the latté kept bleating. Hunched bodies covered most of the floor, too. But sitting against the wall was one skinny guy, alone, with a fair bit of space on either side. Brad quickly sized him up, then advanced on him, looming menacingly, Duane in tow. The skinny guy scrambled up and out of the way. Brad and Duane were able to squeeze into the space he'd left. Brad's right shoulder pressed against Duane's left; squeezed against Duane's right side was some other guy. Right away Brad and Duane started to sweat. They should have taken off their coats when they'd entered; if they got up to do it now, someone might snatch their spot, as they'd snatched it from the skinny guy.

"So," said Brad, looking at Duane and wondering what his own emotions were; he hadn't let himself start feeling them yet. "What's been going on with you?"

"Well. I lost my job."

No shit. It was more than his worn coat, and running into him at the testing center. His unemployed status was written all over him. He was one of *those guys*, now. Same as Brad.

Although frankly Brad thought he was doing better than Duane. Duane had this discombobulated look. And Brad felt like he himself had gotten used to his condition. It had taken time, though. Maybe Duane had only recently joined the ranks of the jobless, in spite of the state of his coat.

For a second they just sat there, then caught each other's eye. It was a novelty, looking someone in the eye like that; at the same time it felt familiar, from the days when they used to hang out. They laughed.

"Shit, man," said Brad. "That sucks about your job." And it did suck. "I'm really sorry, man."

"Oh, it's okay." Duane seemed embarrassed by Brad's sympathy, probably because he'd gotten Brad fired.

"No it's not. What ... I mean, uh, what happened?..." For no good reason he wondered if it might have been something to do with the sexbots and v-brothels. At the thought Brad felt his mouth twisting into a knowing, bitter smile.

But Duane said, "Oh, just what I always worried would happen, is all. Consolidation." Meerville now contained just one mega-school, at least in the public sphere, with tens of thousands of students. "The new school only needs one guidance counselor. And they picked someone else."

Brad nodded. "Gotcha."

With a guilty flush, Duane said, "And, uh ... how about Katie and Keith? How are they liking the mega-school?"

Later, Brad would be touched that Duane had remembered his kids' names. "They actually don't go there," he said. "I actually had to take Katie out of school so that she could do a little part-time work here and there. Help with bills. And with the new place." Thinking about the kind of work Katie had been signed up for was like accidentally opening the door to a soundproofed dungeon and briefly hearing the shrieks within, before managing to slam it closed. But after losing his brotheling gig, Brad had no longer been able to make rent on his old place. With two kids, he'd been able to score a teensy rent-assisted place that technically had no rent; he had to pay such a shit-ton of fees, though, that the new place wound up costing way more per square foot. "And Keith, of course, I mean he's too young to work, legally. But we just couldn't afford the fees for the textbooks and the cafeteria toll and all the other stuff. So we're home-schooling."

Duane presented a politely blank face to this legal fiction. Since every child below ten years old had a legal right to an education, in order to pull Keith from school and thereby escape all its fees, Brad had had to sign a paper assuring the government that he was choosing to home-school his son. But nobody seriously believed that Brad, busy as he was, was really going to set up and enforce some sort of curriculum for his boy. "I'm really sorry about that."

Brad shrugged. Not easy, in this tight space.

Duane said, "I'm really sorry that I got you fired from the brothel."

Until this moment, Brad had never *officially* known that to be the case. He'd *known*, but he hadn't *known*-known. Now his guts turned to jelly and he was freezing again. So much for easing back into their friendship as if nothing had ever happened.

Duane was blinking, fast, forcefully. Brad sympathized. The guy didn't want to break down crying in this jam-packed Starbucks, even though everyone would just ignore him. "I just went crazy," Duane said. "I can't even remember what I was thinking when I made those terrible calls. I remember doing it, but not what I was thinking. Or even how I felt."

"It's cool, man—don't worry about it."

Tears actually began to spill down Duane's haggard face. Brad had lain awake nights, screaming into his pillow and wallowing in visions of Duane crying in remorse for what he'd done. Now, at the sight of it in real life, he wanted to clench his eyes shut and puke. "Please," he said, "*please* don't worry about it. Really."

"I lost you your *job*."

"Well, it was bound to happen anyway."

The misery clotting Duane's face cleared, slightly. "Really?"

"Yeah." This was a lie. Oh, no doubt the brotheling would ultimately have proved as unstable as any job. No doubt they were on the cusp of developing an AI that really could run a sexbot just as well as a human could. In the meantime, though, Brad had been among the best, and he felt confident that even if every single sexbot operator had gotten the axe, he would have gotten it last. But he would lie about that, if it would help Duane stop crying. "I was having all sorts of problems with the company, anyway. If it hadn't been your call, then it would have been something else, pretty soon."

"Really?" Duane obviously smelled bullshit, but he wanted to believe. "But you always seemed so *good* at it."

"Well." Now Brad felt tears pushing at the backs of his own eyes. "You and I kind of, you know. Had a connection, I think."

Duane looked at Brad, contemplating him, a little hushed.

"Anyway," said Brad. They changed the subject. First Brad tried to get Duane to talk about the survival gigs he'd managed to hustle since getting fired, but Duane very clearly didn't want to talk about them (he actually physically winced), so Brad changed the subject again, leading the conversation much the same way he'd always taken charge of their interactions in the v-brothel, without Duane or any other client ever seeming to notice, or at least without them ever seeming to mind. He kept it simple. They talked about the testing facility. That subject required no shameful admissions—each man already knew the other went there—and it offered a gold mine of goofy stories. Soon the two of them were actually making each other laugh, *honestly* laugh, with their descriptions of some of the grotesque characters they'd bumped into, or their interactions with the stubborn, tone-deaf AIs.

This was fun, Brad realized, with awe. When was the last time he'd had any fun? He had to really think about it.... Well, it had been way back at the Meerville Arts Center. Not the last time, when Duane had told him he couldn't help Katie, but the time before that. Honestly, Brad couldn't remember when he'd had fun *before* meeting Duane. Like, in his whole life. He was sure it must have happened, but he couldn't remember it.

Something that had been balled up and twisted inside his chest cavity was opening, unfurling, at last getting room to breathe; he hadn't even known it was constricted; he'd thought his problems were so much bigger, so much more insurmountable. Never in a billion years would it have occurred to him that what he really needed was to call Duane up again, to reconnect with him.... Well, in fairness, he *couldn't* have called him up, since Duane had blocked him. But that would change after today. Brad would sort of casually mention toward the end of their chat that they should start hanging out again, even if it was only to hide out in Starbucks like this—obviously neither could any longer afford the Arts Center. He'd ask if Duane had a new number, ask him to send Brad a text because all Brad's contacts had been wiped after he'd been late with his tablet bill—something like that, anyway. Something to remind Duane that he'd have to unblock Brad, without Brad having to come out and say so.

After a long, increasingly comfortable time of telling funny stories, they reached a lull. Duane sighed, and looked at Brad a touch more seriously. "But, so," he said. "Do you have any, you know. Long-term plans?"

The edges of Brad's vision got a little dimmer, and his airway constricted slightly. He shrugged, keeping shit casual, nonchalant. "You know," he said. "Just keep on trucking. Wait for something to break. Wait for something to happen."

Duane nodded, as if in approval of Brad's sagacity. "Wait for something to change," he put in.

"Something always does," said Brad, then fell silent, embarrassed; it had proven impossible to offer that chestnut without falling into a pompous tone.

Duane kept nodding, working himself up to something. Hopefully a change of subject. Deciding the next time they would hang out was one thing. Otherwise, Brad preferred to avoid talking about the future.

"I've been trying to figure out some new line of work." Duane spoke with a forced, brave cheerfulness. "I mean, we can't just keep going on like *this*, can we?" Duane's hand waved to indicate the Starbucks.

"No," agreed Brad mildly. Obviously they couldn't keep going on like this. Equally obvious was that they would.

Uncomfortable silence from Duane; Brad sensed that he wanted Brad to ask follow-up questions, help lead him to whatever it was he wanted to say. So Brad obliged, already starting to feel sullen and resentful, annoyed. What had happened to that great feeling he'd had? Duane had been leading him out of the grind of his daily hopelessness. Now he wanted to rub his nose in it…. Well, if that was what Duane needed, Brad could try to accommodate. That was part of friendship, too. "Do you have something in mind?"

Duane laughed nervously. "Well, it's not like there are that many jobs *left*, you know."

Yeah, no shit. "Right. But, so. Something in mind?…"

"It's, uh, it's something I should maybe ask *you* for advice about, actually."

Brad couldn't imagine why anyone would ask *him* for advice. "Sure," he said.

"I actually, um, I was actually thinking of trying out for, uh, for the job *you* used to do." He ended with another nervous laugh and a head-shake, as if he just couldn't get over all of life's crazy twists and turns.

Then he saw Brad's ashen face staring at him. Duane's laugh dried up. "Oh, shit," he said. "Look, I…."

"You think anyone can do that job?" said Brad. "Just waltz in and do it?"

"No, of course not, I…. Look, it's just that, like we said, it's one of the only jobs left, and since I already know a little about it from, uh, from the other end…. And then we were talking, and it occurred to me that maybe you might, uh, have some pointers…. Aw, jeez, I can't believe I asked you of all people that. After what I did. I've sunk so low. I'm sorry, it's just, I'm *desperate*…."

"It's not a matter of you being a dickhead for asking me to help you get the job you took from me. It's a matter of, *you can't do it*. Yeah, I know it's one of the only jobs left. You know why?

Because it's one of the few things a computer can't do just as well. Do you think you can out-perform a *computer*?"

Duane didn't reply. Just kept looking at him. His face, which had gotten steadily looser and brighter since they'd bumped into each other, was closing, setting, dimming.

"I was great at that job," said Brad. "Because I meant it. I gave to people, and I liked giving, and they knew it. It doesn't work if you're bullshitting. You think *you* could do that? Do all that stuff, and *really* mean it? *Really* like it?"

Duane replied with the barest shake of his head.

"I did all that, in there. And now it's over. So let's not even talk about it."

They sat a while in silence, Brad fuming, Duane cowed, or offended, or guilty, or whatever he was. The barking grumbling shouting crowd around them went on making its noise.

Brad said, "I gotta go check on my kids." He meant Keith; Katie was at work.

Duane nodded. "I need to go do the pee test."

They left the Starbucks, parting at the door. They didn't touch, only raising their palms in goodbye. They said they hoped to bump into each other again sometime, but no one ever bumps into anyone in Meerville.

ALSO FROM SALTIMBANQUE BOOKS:

IRONHEART, by J. Boyett

Part H.P. Lovecraft and part Alien, Ironheart is the story of what happens when the mining ship Canary comes across a strange derelict on the edge of the galaxy—a derelict occupied by a strange and seemingly immortal woman....

THE SWITCH, by J. Boyett

Beth used to be a powerful witch, till a meth addiction burned her powers away. Her daughter Farrah thinks she's nothing but a loser. But Beth thinks maybe Farrah would change her mind if she had to spend a few days in her mom's shoes—and when she gets her hands on a new source of magic, she decides to make that happen....

DAUGHTER OF THE DAMNED, by J. Boyett

Before Carol was born, Harold ruined her mother's life. Now Carol's out for vengeance, with the help of the bounty hunter Snake.

But her quest has set off a trap left by her mother. And Carol and her mother's old enemy will have to team up, if either wants to get out alive.

THE UNKILLABLES, by J. Boyett

Gash-Eye already thought life was hard, as the Neanderthal slave to a band of Cro-Magnons. Then zombies attacked, wiping out nearly everyone she knows and separating her from the Jaw, her half-breed son. Now she fights to keep the last remnants of her former captors alive. Meanwhile, the Jaw and his father try to survive as they maneuver the zombie-infested landscape alongside time-travelers from thirty thousand years in the future.... Destined to become a classic in the literature of Zombies vs. Cavemen.

COLD PLATE SPECIAL, by Rob Widdicombe

Jarvis Henders has finally hit the beige bottom of his beige life, his law-school dreams in shambles, and every bar singing to him to end his latest streak of sobriety. Instead of falling back off the wagon, he decides to go take his life back from the child molester who stole it. But his journey through the looking glass turns into an adventure where he's too busy trying to guess what will come at him next, to dwell on the ghosts of his past.

STEWART AND JEAN, by J. Boyett

A blind date between Stewart and Jean explodes into a confrontation from the past when Jean realizes that theirs is not a random meeting at all, but that Stewart is the brother of the man who once tried to rape her.

THE LITTLE MERMAID: A HORROR STORY, by J. Boyett

Brenna has an idyllic life with her heroic, dashing, lifeguard boyfriend Mark. She knows it's only natural that other girls should have crushes on the guy. But there's something different about the young girl he's rescued, who seemed to appear in the sea out of nowhere—a young girl with strange powers, and who will stop at nothing to have Mark for herself.

I'M YOUR MAN, by F. Sykes

It's New York in the 1990's, and every week for years Fred has cruised Port Authority for hustlers, living a double life, dreaming of the one perfect boy that he can really love. When he meets Adam, he wonders if he's found that perfect boy after all ... and even though Adam proves to be very imperfect, and very real, Fred's dream is strengthened to the point that he finds it difficult to awake.

BENJAMIN GOLDEN DEVILHORNS, by Doug Shields

A collection of stories set in a bizarre, almost believable universe: the lord of cockroaches breathes the same air as a genius teenage girl with a thing for criminals, a ruthless meat tycoon who hasn't figured out that secret gay affairs are best conducted out of town, and a telepathic bowling ball. Yes, the bowling ball breathes.

RICKY, by J. Boyett

Ricky's hoping to begin a new life upon his release from prison; but on his second day out, someone murders his sister. Determined to find her killer, but with no idea how to go about it, Ricky follows a dangerous path, led by clues that may only be in his mind.

BROTHEL, by J. Boyett

What to do for kicks if you live in a sleepy college town, and all you need to pass your courses is basic literacy? Well, you could keep up with all the popular TV shows. Or see how much alcohol you can drink without dying. Or spice things up with the occasional hump behind the bushes. And if that's not enough you could start a business....

THE VICTIM (AND OTHER SHORT PLAYS), by J. Boyett

In The Victim, April wants Grace to help her prosecute the guys who raped them years before. The only problem is, Grace doesn't remember things that way.... Also included:

A young man picks up a strange woman in a bar, only to realize she's no stranger after all;

An uptight socialite learns some outrageous truths about her family;

A sister stumbles upon her brother's bizarre sexual rite;

A first date ends in grotesque revelations;

A love potion proves all too effective;

A lesbian wedding is complicated when it turns out one bride's brother used to date the other bride.